Ghost Mikawa
Illustration by Hiten
MW01026219
DAYS
with My
STEPSISTER

GOING TO SCHOOL WITH MY STEPSISTER

"What about you? Have you gone anywhere this summer?"
"Hmm? Who, me? You bet! I put on a wicked swimsuit and hung out at the beach, where all the boys hit on me.
Isn't that just what college girls do?"

MY STEPSISTER AT THE POOL

diary

I've been a little scared to write in my diary recently.

Come nighttime, I think about the things that happened during the day, and it's like Asamura is taking up too much space in my brain. When I found out I was moving in with a guy my age I'd never met, I decided I'd do my best to get to know him. And now it's totally backfired. His tastes in food are completely unlike mine, and so are his habits and values. I could've stepped on his toes at any time. I didn't want to be rude or ruin my mom's happiness now that she'd finally found it...

...So I tried hard to learn more about my new family. And then before I knew it, I had started thinking about him constantly.

Every day, I'd see how kind he was in all sorts of situations.

I realized I was looking forward to what new side of him I'd discover that day.

...Even though we promised, at the start, we wouldn't expect things from each other.

Right now, it's still okay. I'm great at hiding my emotions, after all.

Since entering junior high, I've never once cried and asked Mom not to go to work, no matter how lonely I felt. As long as it's just a matter of how I feel, everything should be fine. But what if Asamura starts looking at me like ~~he loves me~~ the same way I look at him? Will I be able to hide my ~~feelings~~ for him?

...I might not be able to. I don't know if my heart is that strong.

I have to draw the line somewhere.

I mean, Asamura is the first person I've

DAYS with My STEPSISTER

3

Ghost Mikawa

Illustration by Hiten

New York

DAYS with my STEPSISTER 3

Ghost Mikawa

Translation by Eriko Sugita ● Cover art by Hiten

GIMAISEIKATSU Vol. 3

First published in Japan in 2021 by KADOKAWA CORPORATION, Tokyo.
English translation rights arranged with KADOKAWA CORPORATION, Tokyo through TUTTLE-MORI AGENCY, INC., Tokyo.

Yen On
150 West 30th Street, 19th Floor, New York, NY 10001

Visit us at yenpress.com • facebook.com/yenpress • twitter.com/yenpress
yenpress.tumblr.com • instagram.com/yenpress

First Yen On Edition: June 2024
Edited by Yen On Editorial: Emma McClain
Designed by Yen Press Design: Wendy Chan

Library of Congress Cataloging-in-Publication Data
Names: Mikawa, Ghost, author. | Hiten (Illustrator), illustrator. | Sugita, Eriko. translation.
Title: Days with my stepsister / Ghost Mikawa ; illustration by Hiten ; translation by Eriko Sugita.
Other titles: Gimai seikatsu. English
Description: First Yen On edition. | New York, NY : Yen On, 2023-
Identifiers: LCCN 2023024502 | ISBN 9781975372033 (v. 1 ; trade paperback) | ISBN 9781975372057 (v. 2 ; trade paperback) | ISBN 9781975372071 (v. 3 ; trade paperback)
Subjects: CYAC: Stepbrothers—Fiction. | Stepsisters—Fiction. | Love—Fiction. | LCGFT: Romance fiction. | Light novels.
Classification: LCC PZ7.1.M5537 Day 2023 | DDC [Fic]—dc23
LC record available at https://lccn.loc.gov/2023024502

ISBNs: 978-1-9753-7207-1 (paperback)
978-1-9753-7208-8 (ebook)

10 9 8 7 6 5 4 3 2 1

LSC-C

Printed in the United States of America

DAYS with My STEPSISTER

"Things would be easy if the whole of humanity could just be chill, like you and me."
Saki Ayase
A high school junior who becomes Yuuta's stepsister after their parents remarry. Her flashy outfits tend to make people think she is a bad girl, and she has a hard time blending in at school.
"You might repay me one day, so it's a win-win."
"Whoa! You must be the big brother Saki's been telling me about! So it is you—Yuuta Asamura from the next class over!"
Maaya Narasaka
Saki's classmate. She's always full of energy and loves to meddle. Unable to bear seeing Saki isolated in class, she cheerfully forced her way into becoming Saki's friend.
Yuuta Asamura
A high school junior. He becomes Saki's older stepbrother after his dad marries Saki's mom. He's an average high schooler, but he distances himself from others. He loves to read and is addicted to books.

Tomokazu Maru

Yuuta's classmate and probably his only friend at school. He's on the baseball team and is a huge nerd.

Taichi Asamura

Yuuta's dad and Saki's stepfather. A lot happened with his first wife, whom he divorced before eventually marrying Akiko Ayase. Taichi gets along well with Yuuta and Saki.

Akiko Ayase

Saki's mom and Yuuta's stepmother. After divorcing her ex-husband, she devoted herself to her work and raised Saki single-handedly until her second marriage.

Shiori Yomiuri

Shiori is a college student who works part-time at a bookstore with Yuuta. She's rooting for him in his relationship with his stepsister.

Days with My Stepsister

Contents

3

Frontispiece and illustrations by Hiten

Our relationship is simple. It's our *hearts* that make it complicated.

● PROLOGUE

It's been one month since summer break began.

For me, Yuuta Asamura, this is my first long vacation since Saki Ayase became my stepsister.

Ayase and I are sixteen, the same age, and we're both second-year students at Suisei High. She's well-known as one of the prettiest girls at our school, and though she's my younger sister, her birthday is only a week after mine.

Now, what would people generally expect to happen in a situation like that?

Due to our parents' marriage, Ayase and I—a girl and a boy right in the middle of puberty—now share a roof and see each other every single day.

And what's more, it's our first summer break together…

If we were a pair of stepsiblings in some run-of-the-mill piece of fiction, I can guarantee we'd be doing all the classic tropes, like going to the pool, the beach, and the summer festival.

We'd hang out together, grow closer, and stumble into a few little incidents that would make our hearts race. That's the natural course of events. It has to be. That's what the readers expect.

But reality is just reality, and it's nothing like fiction. There were no special, exciting developments between Ayase and me.

At least, nothing had happened so far as we approached the end of August and the beginning of September. There was nothing new in our relationship, and the humdrum days passed uneventfully.

That said, we were definitely spending more time together than we had when we were both going to school.

I say that because—

"Good work, Asamura."

"You too, Ayase."

We faced each other and used our surnames like a pair of strangers who had just met.

—for the past month, we'd been working at the same bookstore with exactly the same hours.

● AUGUST 22 (SATURDAY)

It was Saturday morning, halfway into our summer break. Cicadas were chirping noisily outside the window.

A thought occurred to me as I poked into my breakfast omelet with the tips of my chopsticks. Wasn't it kind of a waste to have weekends during break? Couldn't they take all those days and let us exchange them for more time off later?

I didn't think it would be such a big deal. We usually got the following Monday off when a national holiday fell on a Sunday. So then didn't it make sense to give us back all the Saturdays and Sundays we'd lost over break? Or if that was too much to ask, maybe just the Sundays.

I'd felt this way ever since elementary school, and today, I finally broached it at the breakfast table.

My dad looked appalled. "You already have a month off. Is there something you want to do that you need even more time for?"

I stopped moving my chopsticks and thought about it. "…Not in particular."

"Then why?"

"It just seems like I'm being robbed."

"You sound like a little kid."

"I don't think age has anything to do with it."

"When you get to be my age, you don't even know what to do with your days off."

"Come on, you can't say that right in front of Akiko… Wouldn't you like to take the family out or something?"

"Heh-heh. My, Yuuta, you're so thoughtful," Akiko said, "unlike

Taichi." She was sitting across from my dad and gracefully plucking up bits of omelet.

Akiko married my dad two months ago, making her my stepmother. She works as a bartender, so she leaves in the evening and often comes home late at night. On the other hand, Dad works a regular job, so he leaves for work early in the morning and comes home in the evening.

They're newlyweds, but they don't get to spend much time together outside their days off. That's why, when I see them eating breakfast at the same table, it instantly feels like the weekend.

"But you know what, Yuuta?" she continued. "Things are different depending on how you look at them."

"They are?"

"For example, today's Saturday, and we're off, but it's the same as usual for you since you're in the middle of summer break, right?"

I nodded.

It's true that you tend to lose your sense of what day it is during a long vacation like summer break. Maybe not so much at the beginning around the end of July, but after a month or so of living like this, it's inevitable.

"But in fact, today *is* Saturday, not a weekday, and you have work, right?"

"Yeah. I'm working a full shift today, so I'll be gone before noon."

"Good for you. And you worked yesterday, too, right? So you're not doing anything different."

"Uh-huh."

"But since it's Saturday, you'll receive extra pay for working on the weekend!" Akiko declared brightly. "Isn't that great?!"

"Huh? ...What?!"

"Things might seem the same to you, but you still receive that bonus. Don't you feel like you're getting a good deal?"

"Oh yeah... I guess."

"And you wouldn't receive that bonus if all the Saturdays and Sundays during your break were changed out for weekdays. When you look at it that way, don't you think things are best the way they are?"

Now that I thought about it, she was right. I was sure there was something inconsistent about her logic, but her voice was so naturally sincere, I was fully ready to believe her.

"*Sigh.* Asamura, she's duping you," Ayase chimed in. She'd been focusing on eating her breakfast, but it sounded like she couldn't bear listening to any more of this.

"Oh yeah? I had a feeling."

"Yep. By her logic, until today, you've been working during your holidays for regular pay."

"Oh… I see."

Ayase's argument was this: Weekdays during summer break weren't like regular weekdays but more like weekends. When you looked at it that way, it wasn't a good deal at all. In fact, you were losing money five days out of seven.

Akiko had almost convinced me because she'd started out by defining Saturdays during break as "regular days," fixing that definition in my mind. You really have to watch out for people who try to take you for a ride like that.

"Watch out for Mom. She's practically a con artist."

"Now, now, Saki," said Akiko. "That's no way to talk about your mother."

"It's precisely because I'm your daughter that I know what you're really like. It's as easy as pie for you to pull the wool over someone's eyes when you feel like it."

"That brings back memories," Dad said quietly. "Akiko was always good at cheering me up no matter how depressed I was."

If that was Dad's response to what Ayase had just said, didn't that mean he was admitting to being duped? I wasn't sure why he sounded so happy about it.

I supposed it made sense that the woman in front of us would have an easy time fooling someone like Dad or me. She'd worked as a bartender in downtown Shibuya for years and was a master at customer service.

I decided to put all that aside for now, however.

"It's really depressing to think about working for normal pay on my days off," I said. "Convincing myself I'm going to work as normal, but occasionally getting some extra pay for no reason, seems much better for my mental health, so I'll go with that."

Akiko smiled sweetly, then reached out a slender arm and asked, "Would you like some more miso soup, Yuuta?"

"Yes, please."

"Oh, I'll get it. I wanted more, too." Ayase got to her feet before Akiko and snatched away my soup bowl.

"Thanks," I said.

"You're welcome."

"Saki," Dad called out. "Can you get me some more, too?"

"Oh, sure." Holding the ladle in one hand, she turned around and accepted Dad's bowl.

"Thank you, Saki."

"Not at all. Here you go, Asamura."

"Thanks, Ayase."

Ayase served herself last, sat back down, and resumed eating.

"Saki, your miso soup is great as always," Dad said, looking deliriously happy.

On the weekends, Akiko helped Ayase make breakfast, but Ayase had made that morning's soup. It contained the standard ingredients: green onion and fried bean curd. Soaked in the flavor of the miso, the fried-bean-curd pieces were nice and tender and provided a lovely contrast to the texture of the crisp green onions.

"Yeah," I said. "You make really good miso soup, Ayase."

She hesitated for a moment before replying. "…Thanks, Asamura."

Akiko smiled. "Tee-hee. I see the two of you are getting along very well."

"I feel the same," Dad agreed.

Dad and Akiko shared a grin. It was a relief to see them leisurely gazing at each other like that. All my childhood memories of the dinner table were of shouting and screaming, uneasy silences, and cold food.

This was nothing like that. The pair of lovebirds sitting in front of me exchanged words so sweet, it sometimes made me want to throw up. Their teasing made me a little uncomfortable, but it was worth the sacrifice.

Ayase looked fed up, but she was still at the table, which meant she probably felt the same way I did.

"But you still call each other by your surnames. Isn't that weird?" Dad said suddenly.

Akiko turned to Ayase. "Are you still shy about calling him Big Brother? You can just call him Yuuta if that's easier."

I was impressed. Perhaps this was the type of thing that came from experience. I couldn't imagine Ayase sweetly saying the words *Big Brotherrr* ♡, but *Yuuta* wasn't too different from *Asamura*, and it felt closer—more like siblings. Not that I'd ever had a sibling; I was just guessing. But it seemed like a reasonable way for her to address me.

Ayase, however, quietly shook her head. "I'm not feeling particularly shy or anything. It just doesn't feel right..."

"It doesn't?" Akiko pressed.

"No."

"Well, okay," she replied. "And I suppose it's not too confusing."

"Confusing?"

"Before we started dating," Dad said, "Akiko called me Mr. Asamura. If Saki thinks of me as Mr. Asamura and Yuuta as Asamura, we can still avoid it getting too confusing around the house."

I didn't even hear the last part of what he said. I'd frozen up, my mouth hanging open.

I hadn't thought about it before, but Dad had a point. Of course. It was simply good manners, even if they were close. Dad had been Akiko's customer, so as a professional, she couldn't suddenly close the distance between them by calling him *Taichi*.

That was the Japanese way of doing things—at least in public settings. But wait a minute...

"Are you saying you called Akiko *Ms. Ayase* before you guys started dating...?"

"Well, of course I did. Isn't that natural?"

"It took him an awfully long time to start calling me by my given name."

"Ha-ha-ha! You're making me blush," Dad said and scratched his reddened cheeks. He was acting like a teenager, and a feeling of secondhand embarrassment washed over me just looking at him.

We were still eating breakfast, and already, the newlyweds were showing off their love. But I supposed this was what you called a happy family.

I looked up and saw Ayase's brows furrow for an instant as if she was troubled. But soon, she resumed eating with her usual cool expression. This helped me regain my composure, too.

Thanks, Ayase.

I poured coffee and set cups in front of everyone. It was the least I could do since I hadn't helped prepare the meal. Dad and Ayase took their coffee black while Akiko drizzled a little milk in hers.

"Thanks, Yuuta," Akiko said.

"You're welcome."

Incidentally, I change up how I drink my coffee depending on my mood.

Speaking of coffee, for the past month, we'd been having exclusively Brazil Santos or Jamaican Blue Mountain. Dad had bought them in huge quantities back when Ayase was preparing for her retest, after hearing that their aromas enhanced concentration. We had a lot left over, so we were still drinking it.

I wondered whether it was the coffee that had helped me finish my summer homework so quickly or just the knowledge that I'd be busy working.

"I still can't believe Saki got a job at the same bookstore as Yuuta!"

"Mom, how many times have you said that?"

"I was just so surprised."

"It's my first job. It's more efficient to have someone I know there to show me the ropes. Plus, I wanted to read and improve my score in Modern Japanese. That's all."

This was probably the third or fourth time this summer that I'd heard this exchange.

Akiko seemed not to understand, but for Ayase, having to take a retest in Modern Japanese before the break must have been devastating.

To be honest, Ayase's job had surprised me, too. She was supposed to be looking for something easy where she could make a lot of money quickly, but now she was working at a bookstore that didn't pay much and asked a lot of her. And unlike me, she wasn't in it because of how much she loved reading.

When I caught a glimpse of Ayase at the bookstore on the last day of school, I couldn't believe my eyes. She'd never said a thing to me about working there.

I'd wanted to ask her why she'd kept quiet, but I couldn't get away while I was on the clock, and so the question kept bouncing around in my mind. When I got home and she told me right away, it was almost a letdown.

Her answer was simple: *"I'd be embarrassed if I told you and then didn't get hired."*

It was a pretty mundane reason, but I could relate. I would also be embarrassed if I applied for a job I thought looked easy and got rejected.

I took my time drinking my coffee and let my mind wander back to the night Ayase had told me that starting the following day, she would be joining me at my job.

"Are you two okay working all the time like that?"

"It's fine, Dad," I said. "I'm making sure to attend my summer classes. And like I always tell you, I can take care of myself."

As a second-year, I had to start thinking about college entrance exams. Because our school, Suisei High, was especially prestigious, our classmates were talking about nothing but mock exams and summer classes. Unless, of course, they were busy with sports, like my best friend, Tomokazu Maru.

Ayase, however, wouldn't be joining me at my summer classes. The famous prep school that hosted them charged a lot of money, and she'd have to rely on our family's savings to attend.

Dad tried to convince her that it wasn't a problem, but she remained stubborn, and he eventually had to back down.

She was determined to get into a famous college on her own merit and refused to compromise or let anyone help her. I had to respect her grit.

"Summer classes?" Dad replied. "Oh, those don't matter." After blowing off his son's academic concerns (because of his immense trust in me, I hoped), Dad brought up the last thing I'd expected him to be worried about: "It's summer break, and neither of you seem to have gone anywhere fun."

"*That's* your concern?"

Both Ayase and I were busy almost every day, and even family gatherings like this breakfast only happened a few times a month. I was also a little perplexed that a parent would be more worried about their kid having fun than studying, but Dad looked completely serious.

"It's important to enjoy yourselves," he continued. "It isn't easy to get time off to play when you're an adult. You should treasure the ups and downs of your youth and spend time with your friends while you can."

"I could've sworn you two were still 'enjoying your youth' just a minute ago."

"Akiko and I have a mature relationship."

As I watched Dad and Akiko, I began to muse on a philosophical question. What was the difference between children and adults anyway? Maybe it all came down to who was defining it.

"You're high school kids. Don't you want to take trips and join in festivals? You know, go out and have fun?"

"I thought parents were supposed to tell their kids to cut down on the fun and games. Besides, my job *is* fun," I said, exasperated.

Dad shook his head. "It might be fun, but a job is still a job. You need to enjoy your time off."

"I guess, but..."

I always thought most adults saw high schoolers working summer jobs as just enjoying themselves. I knew some did, at least.

But Dad was an exception.

"You'll really have to focus on your entrance exams when you're a third-year, so I think you should have a little more fun while you can."

"I agree," Akiko said. "I worry about Saki, too, since she tends to push herself too hard."

Both Dad and Akiko seemed to have different concerns from the average adult. I'd been thinking it for a while, but the two of them were a lot alike.

"And what about your friends?" she continued. "Don't you think they're lonely?"

Friends, huh…? The image of a muscular guy in glasses popped into my head.

I smiled wryly. "I don't have many friends who'd miss me in the first place, and the only one who would is going through hell on the baseball field right now…"

My best friend, Tomokazu Maru, was the catcher for our school's baseball team. It might be summer break, but he had practice every single day. And that wasn't all—he also had training camp and practice games in other prefectures. Naturally, he didn't have any time to do things with me.

"*I like long breaks,*" he would say to me. "*We have more time to practice!*"

As I recalled Maru's words, I glanced at Ayase. "That's my situation anyway. Ayase's friends seem a little more aggressive, though."

"I have no plans," she replied.

The only friend of hers I knew was Maaya Narasaka, and unlike Maru, I hadn't heard anything about her being swamped with club activities. What's more, she was the mother hen type, and she seemed particularly attached to Ayase. I had a hard time believing that she'd made no invitations over the long summer break.

But Ayase had denied the suggestion so easily that I found it hard to press her on it. Though I was curious, I let it go, and the conversation ended. But later, while I was getting ready for work, I heard a knock at my door.

When I opened it, Ayase was standing in the doorway. She casually said, "Don't worry about Maaya. We aren't the type of friends who go out together during summer break, okay?"

I was at a loss for words. Her tone was so brusque that I started wondering if I'd offended her, and my mind went blank.

"Ayase, wait."

"…What?"

I stopped her on reflex as she turned to go back to her room, but then I couldn't think of what to say. It was hard to explain, but something was bothering me. I felt a precariousness in the way she was acting. My intuition was usually correct, so I didn't want to just let it go.

It was best to nip miscommunication in the bud.

Being friends didn't mean you had to hang out over break, and after three whole months living in the same home, I knew well that Ayase preferred to spend her time on self-improvement rather than going out for fun.

But that didn't mean she was always alone. I'd joined her and Narasaka after school one day and played games, and another time, Narasaka had come over to help Ayase study and even prepared dinner.

The way she was talking now made it seem like the two of them had suddenly drifted apart.

"Sorry," she said at last.

"Huh?!" I panicked. I couldn't believe I'd stopped her and then immediately lost myself in thought.

"I'm sorry if I worried you. It isn't like I'm mad or in a bad mood. Maaya and I just don't really go out together."

"But she came over a couple times."

"She was curious about you. And she'll come over if I ask her to, like last time. She likes to help people out."

I recalled Narasaka saying she had a number of younger brothers. Unlike Ayase and me, who grew up without siblings, she'd probably gotten used to taking care of others.

"But if I don't ask her to come over, she doesn't," Ayase continued. "And I'm the same way."

"Oh. I guess I can understand that. I don't tend to hang out with other people, either."

"You like being alone?"

"I guess I prefer it."

Perhaps it would be more accurate to say I was good at playing by myself. If I felt like it, I could spend hours alone and not mind a bit. In fact, being around others made me anxious. When I was a child, my mother was always upset, and I was constantly worried I would somehow make her mood even worse. Home had never been a relaxing place for me. Maybe that's why I immersed myself in books as a form of escape.

It wasn't just that I was okay spending time alone, either. If I was being honest, being alone was *easier* for me.

"Oh, so you're like me," Ayase replied. "Then I guess there's no need to say anything else."

"Yeah."

"All right, I'm going to get ready for work. I have an errand to run before I get there, so I'll be leaving much earlier."

"Got it." I nodded, but the weird feeling hadn't gone away.

There was something going on with Ayase. I wouldn't say she was *lying*, but the way she was acting felt off. Even after she went back to her room, I kept mulling over what it was, and eventually, a thought occurred to me: Why had Ayase come all the way to my room just to assure me that she wouldn't be hanging out with Narasaka during our break?

I left the apartment a little before noon. That day, my shift ran from afternoon until evening.

I parked my bike in the corner of the parking lot and checked the clock. I had about half an hour until I needed to report to work.

"I'm a little early, but not enough to go anywhere..."

Glancing at the bookstore, I decided to kill a little time inside and walked in through the customer entrance.

All bookstores are generally set up the same way.

The moment you step in, there's a stand meant to catch your eye, piled high with new and trending books stacked so that their covers are showing. It might seem like a lot of customers pass right by, but that's because it's an area with a lot of foot traffic. As I entered the store, I saw a man in his midforties, probably an office worker, look over the stand before heading toward the sports magazines. Even a brief glance like that was well worth the effort.

If a bookstore has just one entrance, then the register is hardly ever far away. The most important thing to a customer who has finished shopping is to be able to quickly move on to their next destination. It was important to spare them the stress of having to walk across the shop after they made their purchase.

Once you've moved past the section for new and trending books, the rest are arranged based on how well they sell. Books that fly off the shelves are closer to the front, and those that tend to hang around are near the back. The general rule is to put books that sell well in places that stand out.

Every bookstore has a certain logic behind how they arrange each section. A more experienced colleague had explained this to me once, and it had been a real aha moment for me.

I thought back to when I'd first started working here. I'd asked Yomiuri, *"If the layout is so important, why do bookstores fiddle around with it so much?"*

It seemed to me that most places tended to shuffle around their various sections every six months or so. I found this extremely irritating, and the bigger the store, the worse the problem. A library would never pull something like that.

"It's such a hassle," I continued, complaining. *"I'll have my eye on some book, and all of a sudden, it vanishes, moved to who knows where."* I was sure any book lover must have felt the same way at least once.

"Yeah. That's exactly why they do it," she said.

Her reply mystified me. *"Huh?"*

"It's like you just said. We move the books around because customers remember where they are."

"What do you mean?"

"Or to be more precise, they only think *they remember. People look at things, but they don't tend to internalize the details. For example, check out this spot on the shelf. Do you remember the name of the book that was here before?"*

She tapped one corner of a line of paperbacks. A book had been sold, and there was an empty space the size of a single volume. We were in the light novel section, which I had looked at many times, but I couldn't remember which book had been there.

"Here's your answer," she said, showing me the cover of a paperback

we'd just gotten back in stock. It was a book that was selling well, written by an author who was good at writing short stories—a rarity these days. I'd read it, of course, and even though it wasn't part of a series, I should have noticed that books by the same person were on either side of the empty space.

"Oh, this."

"You looked at this shelf a minute ago and didn't notice anything different about it, did you?"

"Well…that's true."

"In other words, you don't remember what was on the shelf. But your brain thinks it's the same as usual. Humans are just animals, you know. And animals tend to lose focus when they perceive that nothing's changed."

I groaned. She'd just used me to prove her point, so her argument was especially convincing. I saw a small grin forming on her face. At a glance, Yomiuri looked like an old-fashioned Japanese beauty—all elegance and reserve—but in reality, she was something of an oddball.

"So that's how it is."

"Yep. People get it in their heads that nothing's changed, and so there's no need to pay attention. Bookstores are trying to crush that false sense of complacency, so every once in a while, they switch things around. Then customers have to search for what they want again, forcing them to pay more attention. Unlike a library, bookstores are running a business. If customers only look at the new-books stand, then what's the point of everything else? If they don't shuffle around the remaining shelves, they die. I can think of a bunch of bookstores that let their shelves go stagnant and rot, and not one of them is still around."

"Thank you for your thoughtful and philosophical explanation."

"I'm pretty cool, huh?"

"I was reminded of a hundred-year-old man with a white beard like you see in RPGs."

"Hmph. That doesn't sound very cool." Yomiuri pouted her lips and sulked.

Thinking back to what she said that day, I glanced from the new-books stand to the shelves behind it.

I've always felt that bookstores are like showcases of human knowledge. New publications reflect the flow of time, and you can really get a sense of what's going on in the world just by looking at their titles and covers. It was my favorite way to kill time.

I passed by the stand and began circling the store, checking out the new books and making sure to run my eyes over the spines lined up on the shelves. This helped me get a good grasp of what was in the store, which would help me deal with customer queries once I started working.

After touring around the shelves, I figured I might as well change into my work uniform. Just as I started to head to the back, someone tapped me on the shoulder from behind.

"Hey, Yuuta."

I turned around and saw Shiori Yomiuri, still wearing casual clothes.

"Hey, don't surprise me like that," I said. "You almost gave me a heart attack."

"Is your heart that delicate?"

"It may not look that way, but yeah."

"I'll believe you if you take it out and show it to me."

"Only if you promise to put it back exactly as it was."

She laughed at that. "A bargain right out of Shakespeare. Even I know you can't take out someone's heart without shedding a little blood, so I guess I'll have to take your word for it."

"Good."

I looked a little closer and saw that Yomiuri was clad in a sleeveless white top and skinny jeans, with her black hair tied up in loose pigtails. Her bare neck gave off a cool, refreshing vibe.

"You're pretty early, aren't you?" she said.

"So are you." I'd thought Yomiuri was on the same shift as Ayase and me.

"It's boring at home, and the store has good air-conditioning. I thought I'd take a look around before heading to the back."

"You had nothing better to do?"

"College kids are like that."

"No seminars or clubs? No research to finish?"

"La, la, la! I can't hear a word you're sayiiing!"

"Please don't act like a grade schooler. How old are you anyway?"

"Don't you know? They say it's better to act younger than your age instead of older."

"Now you're making up sophisms like a junior high schooler."

"A leopard cannot change its spots. We're all the same people as we were in grade school."

"Your words might sound deep, but aren't you just making up excuses for being lazy…?"

"You'll understand once you start college. College students aren't as grown-up as high school kids think." She grinned. I had to admit, she was pretty convincing. "Where's your little sister today, by the way?"

"I don't know… Is she not here yet? She left before I did, so she should arrive pretty soon."

I had never once come to work with Ayase. She'd suggested we continue to draw a line between our public and private lives, just like with school, and I'd agreed.

That said, it wasn't like there'd be a problem if people found out we were siblings. The store manager had seen our résumés, so he already knew. We just didn't feel like blabbing about it to the other employees.

Besides, I rode my bike, while Ayase walked. If we wanted to come to work together, one of us would have to change the way we did things, and neither of us was keen to put in that kind of effort.

"To think that your sister's working here, too! Hey, why are you looking at me like that?"

"Oh, nothing… We were just talking about something similar at home."

Was it that surprising to everyone that Ayase was working at the bookstore?

Yomiuri flashed me a pensive look. "I don't think it's that weird, but high school kids usually want to spend their time having fun. Your sister seems just like you, though—all about work."

"You think so? What about you? Have you gone anywhere this summer?"

"Hmm? Who, me? You bet! I put on a wicked swimsuit and hung out at the beach, where all the boys hit on me. Isn't that just what college girls do?"

Why did she sound so proud of herself?

And what was a "wicked" swimsuit anyway? Objectively speaking, Yomiuri was very pretty. As long as she kept her mouth shut, she looked like the picture of a traditional Japanese beauty, with her graceful figure and long black hair. Inside, though, she was more like a middle-aged man.

"You went to the beach?" I asked.

"Why do you look disgusted?"

"I'm not disgusted… It's just, when I think of the beach, all I see are huge crowds."

Was it even possible to find a beach on the mainland where you could swim without wading through a sea of people? As an introvert, I didn't do well in that kind of environment.

"That's okay. I didn't go to the beach to swim."

"Then you just went to meet guys?"

"Yep. Exactly."

"What's so great about guys flirting with you?"

"They buy me free meals."

"But you have an income…"

Then again, you couldn't make all that much working part-time at a bookstore. Selling books wasn't all that profitable, which meant that salaries were low. Even full-time employees had it bad, and it was only worse for part-timers.

"Oh? Don't you like free meals?" she asked.

"I don't like owing people. And when someone treats me, it's like they're implying I can't earn enough by myself. I don't like how it makes me feel."

As a guy who saw the world in terms of give-and-take, getting something for free only made me uneasy. Food always tasted better when I'd bought it with my own money.

"Well, that's probably a good way to be. But in my case, they're getting to see a lovely female college student in a bathing suit, so it's an even exchange. Just think of all that youthful skin on display."

"Youthful skin…? You sound more like a dried-up old man."

"Are you calling me a dried-up husk?"

"I'm not." *I'm just thinking it.*

"So you're just thinking it."

"Sorry."

"By the way," Yomiuri said, placing her index finger against her lips and grinning like a cat that'd gotten away with being naughty. "Everything I just said was a lie."

"…Everything?"

"Yeah, everything."

"Why did you lie?"

"No reason!" she said with emphasis.

Now that I knew she'd made it all up, it seemed obvious. Her bare white arms and pretty face were as pale as ever, without the barest hint of a tan.

"Jokes aside, work's starting soon," she said. "So why don't we go and get changed?"

We headed to the back of the store, then split up. I proceeded to the men's changing room and put on my work uniform.

I was about to enter the back office when Yomiuri and Ayase stepped out of the women's changing room together. It appeared the latter had shown up right on time.

She was wearing her apron—an outfit I'd seen numerous times since break began. She wore her hair differently than she did at home or at school: a simple, functional ponytail tied with a bow. The long, narrow gathering of hair resembled the tail of a majestic horse. Maybe it was the contrast of the basic uniform with her flashy hair, but despite how often I saw her, my gaze was drawn to her like a magnet.

For a moment, our eyes seemed to meet. But it lasted less than a second, and she quickly looked away.

Come on, Yuuta, get used to her, for crying out loud. I scolded myself and corrected my posture. If I kept staring at her like that, I'd only creep her out.

Perhaps because it was a Saturday and school was on break, the store had been packed since around noon. Around three o'clock, however, there was a lull.

Ayase had just rung up a customer's sale, thanked them cheerfully, and seen them out. After that, no one else lined up at the register. Ayase, Yomiuri, and I were standing behind the counter, and we heaved a collective sigh of relief.

"Ayase, you're a fast learner," Yomiuri said. "To think you've only been here a month!"

"Really?"

"Yep. Your brother was pretty impressive, too. But I think you might surpass him!"

She sounded like she really meant it. I felt the same way. Ayase was skilled at handling the cash register and dealing with customers. I didn't even need to back her up anymore, and she'd mastered just about everything within a week. I certainly didn't remember catching on so quickly.

Just then, I realized something. Yomiuri referred to Ayase as "your little sister" when speaking to me but called her Ayase while on the job. It was little things like that that made her seem mature—not age-wise, but emotionally.

"Thank you," Ayase replied with a smile.

Since I mostly saw her at home these days, I was used to the cool, aloof persona she maintained in private. It had been a while since I'd witnessed her put on this kind of public-facing smile. It reminded me of what she'd looked like when we first met at that restaurant with our parents.

"It's all because I had such a great teacher," she continued.

"Even your response is perfect!" Yomiuri gushed.

"No, I really mean it."

"Um...," came a woman's voice.

"Oh, sorry, ma'am!"

Ayase quickly responded to the next customer approaching the register. She plastered a perfect smile on her face and jumped in to help the elegant older woman, who appeared to be searching for a manga.

"Shall I take over the cash register for you?" I asked.

"Yes, please," said Ayase as she headed out onto the sales floor.

I thought she'd be back right away, but after ten minutes, she still hadn't returned. I was a little worried about her, but customers had started queuing, and I couldn't get away.

Ayase wasn't a big reader, and she didn't consume much manga, either. Maybe she'd gotten lost trying to help the customer.

Yomiuri tapped me on the shoulder. She must've seen the concern on my face. "I'll handle the cash register. You go help her."

I thanked her and took off. On my way to the manga section, I spotted Ayase wandering around with the older woman.

"Ayase. Did you find what you were looking for?"

"Asamura..."

When she turned around, I saw that her eyebrows were lowered like she was at a complete loss.

The customer was quite elderly, and it seemed she was there to buy a book for her grandchild. She probably didn't know much about manga, either, and she appeared a bit uneasy.

The book they were searching for was a new work that had just come out that month. It had recently been announced that it would be made into an anime, and we anticipated good sales. We'd ordered quite a few, so it couldn't have sold out. And yet they hadn't been able to find it.

"Considering the publisher, this should be the right shelf...," Ayase said.

"Did you look it up in the system?" I asked, glancing at a computer in one corner of the store. It should've had information on everything in stock.

"It said we have more than five copies left. But..."

"It wasn't on the stand up front, was it?"

"No. We checked."

After catching up on the situation, I started thinking. It didn't make sense that she wasn't able to find a new release that just came out this month. It was selling well, but our records said we had copies available.

And yet, like Ayase had said, I didn't see it on the stand with all the colorful POP displays.

I scanned the spines on the shelf, which was filled from top to bottom with books from the same publisher. Checking through each book arranged by author name, I found other volumes from the series but not the latest one. Apparently, the ones on the shelf had already sold.

"It isn't here…," I said.

"No. But it should be."

"In that case… Hmm. Maybe around here… Yeah, this looks suspicious."

I lifted the top book in a stack of new releases. Below it was another completely different book—the very one we were looking for.

"Oh!"

"Here it is," I said. "This is the one you wanted, right?"

When customers picked up our books, they often didn't return them to the right place. That was what had happened here. We would have noticed it immediately if Ayase or I had been the one to set out the books or if the customer had put it down more carelessly. But when the stack looked neat, it was hard to tell. There were five copies of the manga under the misplaced book, which matched our records.

"Wow…!" Ayase exclaimed. "How did you know it was there?"

"Just a feeling. But never mind that—your customer is waiting."

"Oh, right. Um…ma'am, is this the book you're looking for?" Ayase turned to the customer and showed her the manga.

The woman accepted the book and smiled happily. "Yes, yes. I think this is it."

"Will that be all?"

The lady nodded, and we took her to the register. She paid for the book, tucked it away in her bag like a treasure, then bowed deeply and headed out.

Ayase and I exhaled in relief.

"I'm glad you found her book," she said. "But how'd you do it…? It was like you have ESP."

"It was nothing, really."

The POP display had a sticker reading ON SALE AUGUST 21, and I knew the publisher of the top book had a different sales schedule. For that reason, it had seemed out of place to me.

"I didn't notice…"

Ayase probably didn't think much about launch dates for manga, unlike me, a bookworm by nature who looked forward to new releases.

"It's tough if you don't know what to look out for. I have a bit more experience—that's all."

I thought back to what Yomiuri had said way back when.

"Animals tend to lose focus when they perceive that nothing's changed."

Preconceptions make things right in front of you invisible.

"I'm still impressed," Ayase said.

"Yomiuri would have found the book even sooner."

The girl in question had headed back to the sales floor as soon as Ayase and I returned to the register.

"Oh," Ayase mumbled as she prepared to ring up more purchases.

Business was picking back up, and a line of customers had begun to form.

I could see the moon shining through the gaps between buildings.

There were about ten days left of August. The wind felt lukewarm against my skin, and the heat rising from the asphalt sidewalk, left over from the afternoon, seemed to suffocate me.

It was almost a quarter past ten at night. High schoolers were only allowed to work until ten, and we had to be completely off the floor by then. So in effect, work ended at nine fifty.

That said, it had taken me until now to put my stuff together and leave the store. Ayase had finished at the same time, and we were walking together side by side.

We didn't like coordinating and came to work separately at whatever times suited us. So why did we always go home together, you ask?

There was a reason, as it happened: Akiko insisted. That was her sole condition for allowing her daughter to work so late. She didn't want Ayase to walk home alone through Shibuya at night.

At first, Ayase objected. She said it was ridiculous for Akiko to think she needed her brother as a bodyguard just because she was a girl. In the past, she had walked alone late at night through the city whenever she had to visit Akiko at work, so she couldn't understand why her mother was so worried.

All this reminded me of the rumors about Ayase dating for money. Someone must have seen her out late on her way to visit Akiko. It finally made sense.

And there was probably another reason why Ayase didn't want to walk back with me: I could get home a lot faster on my own by riding my bike. She probably didn't want to force me to match her pace. I would have felt the same way in her shoes. After all, her policy was to give a lot when it came to give-and-take.

But in the end, she agreed to Akiko's condition on the grounds that she was still her dependent, and it would be selfish to make her worry unnecessarily.

I was a little relieved to hear that. No matter how much she insisted that she was fine on her own, I didn't really want her walking home alone through downtown Shibuya at night. If she was making the trip every day, instead of just an occasional visit to her mother, her chances of running into trouble would surely increase. When I told her as much, she casually agreed with me.

And that was how Ayase and I ended up walking home together.

I wiped the sweat dripping down my chin as we wove our way through the crowds. It didn't seem to have cooled down at all since the afternoon.

"Summer's still going strong, huh?" I said.

"It's already autumn…," Ayase said at the same time.

"Huh?"

"What?"

We both stopped in our tracks. Ayase looked at me in shock, and I met her gaze uncertainly. Then after watching me for a moment, she nodded.

"Were you talking about the heat?" she asked.

"Yeah. What about you?"

"I was talking about that," she said, jerking her chin toward a boutique next to a pedestrian bridge. She seemed to be indicating the display window.

On the other side of the glass was a row of mannequins.

"That's autumn?"

"Yeah. I mean, it is, isn't it?" She looked even more shocked when I tilted my head, puzzled. "What?! You really don't get it?"

"Sorry. I can't tell the difference between the clothes you're wearing and the stuff on the mannequins."

Now that she mentioned it, I could tell they weren't displaying clothes meant for the middle of summer. The sleeves seemed a little long for that... probably.

But Ayase wasn't wearing short sleeves, either—she had on a gingham checked shirt over a knit tank top.

"That's not what I'm talking about. You can tell right away that the colors and accessories are all the latest new styles for autumn. In fact, it's been ages since any of these stores have had their mannequins in summer clothes. More importantly, those mannequins were wearing different clothes just yesterday."

"They were?"

"You're kidding..."

"I'm not saying I don't believe you. I'm sure you know what you're talking about. I just wish you'd stop looking at me like I'm Santa Claus or a zombie."

"You're way weirder than that. If Santa or a zombie showed up right now, I wouldn't even bat an eye."

"Hey, you're hurting my feelings."

She was treating me like an animal off the IUCN Red List or a cryptid. Was I crazy for thinking she was the weirder one? How many people could remember what some mannequins were wearing the day before?

"Do you really have no interest in fashion?" she asked.

"Have you ever seen me reading a fashion magazine?"

A book lover like me would much rather spend their money on books than on clothes. And anyway, what good would it do for me to get dressed up when I'm such an introvert? Who was I trying to impress? When I said this to Ayase, she nodded.

"I see… So when you aren't interested, you really don't notice anything."

"Apparently not."

"I guess there's no problem, since you don't seem like you want to work at a clothing shop or anything…"

"…Huh? What are you talking about?"

"Nothing…," she said curtly and picked up her pace.

With no clue what she was thinking, I pushed my bike and rushed to catch up with her.

For whatever reason, she seemed to be in a good mood after that.

● AUGUST 23 (SUNDAY)

The heat woke me up that morning.

I checked the alarm clock by my pillow and saw it was…three—no, four minutes after ten. It was the last week of August, but the summer heat seemed like it would never leave.

I remembered Akiko saying you could get heatstroke indoors and quickly turned on the air conditioner. Then, since I'd gotten sweaty, I changed clothes. When I finally opened the door to the living room, I was engulfed by a suffocating wave of heat. I could barely breathe.

Dad was standing on a stepladder, checking the air conditioner. Akiko stood next to him, looking worried. It was Sunday, but it was pretty rare to see Dad and Akiko in the living room together two days in a row. Something was up.

Dad glanced over at me. "Oh, Yuuta. Good morning."

"Good morning, Yuuta."

"Good morning. Um, is there something wrong with the air conditioner?"

"It stopped working a little while ago. I was playing around with it and ended up waking Akiko."

"Want me to help?"

"Oh, no, it's okay. I'm not repairing anything; I'm just taking a look. An amateur like me can't hope to fix an air conditioner."

He had a point.

Dad checked the error messages on the display and compared them to the manual, then flicked the on-off button on the remote control to change the operation mode, but no cool air came out of the device.

"This is our oldest unit," he said. "Maybe we need to buy a replacement."

"And you just bought one for Saki's room…," Akiko added. "I'm sorry, Taichi."

"Hey, it's nobody's fault. We were using that room for storage, so it didn't need to be cooled before. But Saki can't study without an air conditioner, can she?"

"Thank you, Taichi."

As I listened to their exchange, I realized that Ayase wasn't in the living room.

"Is Ayase in her room?" I asked.

"Yes. She was watching Taichi until a minute ago, but she said it was too hot. She's not good with heat."

"Oh."

"It was a nightmare when she was young. She'd beg for ice cream, make a fuss about going to the pool…"

I remembered that photo of her as a child—the one Dad showed me before he and Akiko got married. She'd looked like a lively elementary schooler. These days, she seemed comparatively relaxed. It was hard to imagine her as a kid, making a fuss and begging her mom to take her out.

"She became easier to handle as she got older, but I kind of miss those days."

"I wonder if all kids stop wanting to hang out with their parents around puberty," Dad said. "Yuuta was like that, too."

Akiko looked down and sighed. "In Saki's case, it didn't take that long… By the time she entered junior high school, she was already the way she is now."

Akiko was being vague, but I could more or less imagine what had happened.

Ayase had told me that it was around then that things got tense at home; her dad stopped coming home, and Akiko began working. She must have sensed the situation despite her young age and stopped causing extra stress.

"Sorry, I didn't mean to probe," Dad said.

Akiko smiled. "It's okay." She didn't seem bothered by the subject, but Dad looked embarrassed. *Come on, Dad. You aren't helping Akiko by getting all flustered up there on the stepladder.*

I'd had no idea that Ayase liked going to the pool when she was young… I had a hard time imagining her frolicking happily in the water. I wondered if she'd still enjoy it, if all her cares disappeared and she could do whatever she wanted.

As an introvert and a homebody, I didn't really like the idea of big crowds or tiring myself out with exercise.

"Hmm. It seems like it's really broken. I should probably call for repairs, but it's the busy season for stuff like this, so who knows when they'll be able to send someone?"

"What a predicament… Oh, be careful on your way down, dear."

"Yuuta, you should spend the day in your room."

"Okay." Naturally, I had the evening shift that day.

I asked Dad and Akiko what their plans were. Akiko said she wanted to go shopping, and Dad said he would tag along so he could carry everything for her.

I hadn't considered going out—that sounded like a pretty good idea.

Akiko said she would tell Ayase about the situation and headed into the kitchen. "Yuuta, do you want a bite to eat? I'm about to whip up something for myself."

"Oh, sure. Thanks."

Dad and Ayase had already finished breakfast, so Akiko reheated the leftovers for us. Dad opened the door to their bedroom, trying to bring in some cool air, but it was like a drop in the bucket, and soon, I was sweating like a pig. It was at times like this that I longed for an electric fan.

After we finished breakfast and put away the dishes, I grabbed a drink from the fridge and went back to my room, just as Ayase had.

Now what?

It was around noon, and I was flipping through the pages of a book I was reading, wondering what Ayase was up to, when Maru called my cell phone. He asked what my plans were for that afternoon, and I told him I didn't have any, so he asked me to come shopping with him.

Reluctant to go out in the heat, I was just about to turn him down when I remembered I'd have to stay locked up in my room all day. With that in mind, I decided to go.

A little later, I was standing in front of Shibuya Station. It was a lot busier downtown on the weekend than it was during the week. As I watched the waves of people churn past, the heat seemed to increase exponentially.

I'd parked my bike in my usual spot near the train station. That seemed easiest, since I was working that evening.

Maru wanted to go to a store that sold anime merchandise. They also sold manga and light novels, which meant they were my workplace's competitor—not that it mattered. And our store didn't sell anime merchandise anyway.

I walked north along Jingu Street and turned west at Inogashira Street. At some point, the road forked, and I proceeded up Udagawa Street. That's probably the easiest way to describe my route. It may sound far to someone who isn't familiar with Shibuya, but the bustling cityscape provided a nice distraction.

Some group was using vacant space on the street to provide free samples for a new canned juice drink. Elsewhere, a girl at a temporary stand outside a shop was promoting their most popular products. When I let myself take in the sights around me, I always seemed to arrive at my destination in no time.

I was five minutes early for my meeting with Maru.

"Hey. Thanks for coming." Tomokazu Maru—my best friend—saw me and walked over. He was sporting a tan from all that baseball practice.

"Hey, it's been a while. No afternoon practice today, huh?"

"Nope. Only in the morning. Nonstop practice isn't popular these days. Tiring yourself out in this heat will only result in sickness and injury. You gotta rest up when you can—that's the modern way to train."

"I see."

Each practice was probably pretty grueling, so it wasn't in the coach's interest to overwork the team only to have the players injure themselves.

"Sorry for making you come out here in this heat."

"Actually…"

I told Maru about our broken air conditioner and explained that I'd chosen to go shopping with him because it was just as hot at home. I figured if I was honest, he wouldn't have to feel guilty.

"What a disaster. Okay, first, I'd like to get what I came for before it sells out."

"Okay."

Maru didn't usually involve other people in his hobbies. If he'd asked me to come, he had to have a good reason—he wanted two of something that had a limit of one per customer. If he went alone, he'd have to visit several stores, which he didn't have time for. Apparently, this particular item had gone on sale three days ago, so I understood his concern that it might sell out.

Once I promised to do something, I intended to do my best to make it happen. I was ready to buy whatever he was after… At that point, I realized I still didn't know what the item was.

"Once we've completed our objective, we can grab a bite somewhere if we're hungry."

"Sounds good."

I'd been to the manga and light novel corners in this store several times, but since I wasn't that interested in merchandise, I had Maru show me the way.

"So what's this anime about?"

Maru explained as he hurried ahead. It appeared he was after some merchandise for an anime that had aired in the spring. The show was over now, but popular anime often received additional merchandise later on. I remembered the anime he was talking about—it was a slice-of-life story about a group of five guys and girls.

"The thing I want is the robot."

"What?"

I didn't understand what he was saying. Wasn't that anime about a bunch of teenagers living in a quiet country town surrounded by nature?

"Don't you remember? The light novel the protagonist was reading in episode five was science fiction."

"Oh…"

It all came back to me. Recently, nerd culture had reached the mainstream, and cheerful nerd types were often included in the character lineups of shows, either as a protagonist or a side character… I recalled the character in question being a big fan of some battle-heavy sci-fi series with little to no relationship to the main plot.

"Wait, don't tell me…"

"The robot is from the sci-fi series the protagonist likes."

"That's really pushing it for anime merchandise. That robot's not even in the show!"

"But it's so cool," Maru said before naming the illustrator who had designed it. He looked flabbergasted when I said I'd never heard of them. He then launched into an eloquent speech about how ignorant I was.

"So anyway," I said, "they're releasing a toy replica of that robot, huh?"

"Precisely."

When we reached the right part of the shop, we saw were in luck—the toy robot was still available. And we'd arrived just in time, because after we took two, only one was left.

We took our robots to the register and got in line. Since it was Sunday, the shop had a lot of customers, so it was going to be a long wait. We moved to the end of the line and continued our discussion as it slowly inched forward.

"I see what you mean," I said. "This robot *is* pretty cool."

"Told you so."

I was no expert in toy robots, but even this one's packaging looked great. The toy sat in a big box about fifty centimeters tall, plastered with a logo for the fake series it was supposed to come from. The logo for the anime was much smaller and located off in a corner. It made it hard to tell which show the toy was from, but I liked how it made it seem as though the robot's series really existed in our universe.

"It has a whole bunch of moving parts, too. It'll be a blast to play with."

"You're going to play with it…?"

"Oh? Never played with robot or monster toys before?"

"I guess I have but not very often."

I could understand displaying and admiring them, but I didn't get why people would want to play with them. I was more into reading manga and novels than watching anime anyway.

When I was little, I'd assembled and displayed a few plastic-model warships my dad had collected. But after my birth mother got mad at me and tossed them out, saying they were just clutter, I'd vowed never to do it again. It might have made a fun hobby if I'd had a more understanding family.

Manga and novels were much easier. I could hole up in my room and read them, and because they just looked like books, it was harder for my mother to notice.

"Oh, Asamura," Maru said, suddenly changing the subject. "I heard you were going to the pool with Narasaka and her friend. Is that true?"

When I heard that, my brain froze over. Who was going to a pool with whom now?

Apparently not noticing my confusion, he added, "You sly dog. I look away for one second, and you're going out on dates."

"Wait! What are you talking about?"

"What do you mean? I'm talking about you, Ayase, and Narasaka going to the pool."

"This is the first I'm hearing about it."

I didn't even know which pool he meant.

I was confused, and it must have shown on my face.

Maru told me he'd heard about the invite through his friends on the baseball team. According to them, Narasaka was planning on going to the pool with some of our classmates, both boys and girls, and Saki Ayase and Yuuta Asamura were two of the names on her list.

"Hasn't she asked you to go yet?"

"Nope. I haven't even talked to her since break started."

"Hmm. Maybe you'll get an invite soon."

"It's almost the end of August."

"That shouldn't be a problem since it's still so hot."

"I…guess you're right."

I'd had no idea a plan like that was in the works… Was I even close enough friends with Narasaka to score that kind of invite? I could count the number of times we'd talked on one hand. I knew she was a bold, sociable person, but this was way beyond my imagination.

Oh well. There was no guarantee she'd end up asking me. This was secondhand information, after all.

Soon, Maru and I reached the front of the line. We paid for our robots and headed back toward the train station along the same route we'd come. When we were almost to the bookstore where I worked, we found a café and stepped inside.

We both ordered iced coffees.

Maru got a large club sandwich as well. He was an athlete, so he ate a lot.

The coffee cost almost double what it would have at a fast-food joint, but it was worth the price to be able to sit comfortably in a nice chair. That said, this particular café was part of a chain and was only a little more stylish than fast food. It was the kind of place where regulars placed impenetrable orders that sounded like arcane curses, though Maru and I meekly placed a much more normal order.

Compared with an authentic coffee shop, however, which would have increased the price by an entire digit, this kind of place was a little more suited to a high school student's budget.

I'd once stepped into a place near Shibuya Station without looking at the menu posted outside and left right away after seeing the prices. The whole thing had been terribly embarrassing, but four digits for a cup of coffee was way too much for me.

Maru and I set our trays on the table and sighed.

"So why did you need two of those robots?" I asked, glancing at our paper bags.

"One is for regular use, and the other is for safekeeping, of course."

"Oh, you mean it's not for proselytizing?"

"...You already knew, didn't you? That's low, Asamura."

"I didn't, though I had a hunch. I just remembered you saying you had someone you gave presents to."

I also knew that some people bought multiples of items they really liked. But if you asked me, Maru wasn't the type to call on a friend to help him buy something just so he could have two of them. He must have had some reason that he needed to get two robots, even if it meant owing me.

"Actually, someone asked me to get it."

"Someone asked you to?"

"Yeah. An online friend. They wanted one but couldn't get to a store during the sales period, so I promised I'd buy one and send it to them."

"Oh."

I hadn't known Maru had a friend like that.

He told me how they'd met in an anime chat room. They'd hit it off, and they would share recommendations and send each other goods for things they knew the other was interested in.

Since they sent each other items, they must have shared addresses. And yet they didn't know each other's names, only their respective social media handles. That struck me as pretty typical of a modern friendship. From their address, Maru knew they lived somewhere close by in the city, but he said they'd never met.

"I would think that as like-minded souls, you'd be running into each other at offline meetings. In fact, that seems like the kind of thing *you'd* be trying to organize."

Offline meetings were physical gatherings as opposed to online. While you could meet with someone anytime over the internet, humans tended to want to see each other face-to-face sometimes, too. Maru had the necessary planning skills and initiative, and he seemed like the type to act as soon as the idea struck him. Although he was probably limited by his baseball practices, which continued through the weekend.

"Not a good idea," he said.

"Why not?"

"It's not everyone, of course, but casual offline events tend to attract guys looking to pick up girls. You'd need to be careful to limit participants to those you trust, or you'd be inviting trouble. At least, that's how I'd feel if I were organizing one."

"That's very cautious of you. Wait, picking up girls? …Is this friend of yours a girl, by any chance?"

"According to her, yes. She's a college student."

"A college student… So she's older than us."

Yomiuri's face flashed through my mind. She was the only college girl I knew. It wasn't common for high schoolers like Maru and me to meet college girls, and yet it turned out both of us knew one. What a funny coincidence.

But thinking about it, it was probably rarer to meet someone your own age online.

"Judging by her posts, she seems really intelligent. She has a lot of knowledge, and it isn't focused in one area, like mine. We have good, meaningful conversations, and it helps that she's positive, no matter who she's dealing with."

"Huh. She sounds like the type a lot of people would want to get closer to… I think I understand why you're being careful now."

"Yeah. She's pretty popular in the chat room."

If Maru were to host an offline meeting, a lot of guys might show up hoping to get a date with her.

"I'm impressed you got to the point of sending each other anime merchandise."

"Yeah, it happened by coincidence. I'll tell you all about it some time."

"I can't wait. So have you fallen for her?"

Maru looked a little shocked. He probably hadn't expected me to ask a question like that.

"Oh, uh…not particularly."

What an unusual response. He was always teasing me about things like that, so I'd figured I might as well get one in while I had the chance.

I wanted to ask, "Really?" but Maru looked genuinely embarrassed and started mumbling vaguely. Eventually, he excused himself, saying he had to use the bathroom.

This, from Maru…?

I wondered if this girl was the same person he sent presents to. I considered us best friends, but it occurred to me then that there was still a lot

about Maru's life I didn't know. I'd assumed that, like me, he wasn't very interested in romance.

Romance, huh? I enjoyed romantic comedy novels, but I'd always read them as a bystander, merely observing other people's lives. I never imagined a situation like that happening to me.

How could it? This was reality. Some cute girl wasn't just going to fall out of the sky and date me...unless my dad happened to marry a woman with a daughter my age and we started living together, I supposed. Though that didn't guarantee she'd be cute—though she was, of course. There was no arguing that.

Wait a minute. Who was I imagining just now?

It was true that Ayase was cute, but she was my younger sister.

"Asamura?"

She had a cute voice, too, just like that. But she was still my sister, and— *Huh?!*

I turned around and saw a girl with light-colored hair standing in the aisle by our table and looking at me. This was no hallucination—it was Ayase.

"What are you doing here...?" I asked.

"This is the closest coffee shop to the bookstore."

"Oh...I see."

This shouldn't have come as a surprise. We worked at the same bookstore and were on the same shift, and since this coffee shop was the best place to kill time, there was a high chance of running into her here. She had come for the exact same reason I'd suggested the place to Maru. It was practically inevitable.

Still, it caught me by surprise. What was I supposed to say now?

"Okay, I'll be on my way," she said.

"Huh?"

My brain, which had been spinning idly, was forced to reboot. By the time I regained my bearings, I was vacantly watching Ayase walk away.

She was dressed for the summer, in a one-shoulder top and light-blue shorts. *She sure has a high waist; it makes her look like a model. Oh, she's*

wearing sneakers today. That's unusual. I wonder if she wore them to go with her outfit. She walked away breezily; the door opened for her, then closed.

"Sorry to keep you waiting."

"Huh?! Oh, Maru."

"I thought it might be time for you to go to work and rushed back, but… Asamura? Wasn't that Ayase you were talking to?"

What time was it? I looked at the clock and saw that my shift was about to start. Oh, so that was why Ayase took off.

"There's something going on between you and Ayase, isn't there?" Maru said suspiciously.

"Oh, uh… Not really."

I'd be a great big liar if I tried to say no at this point. Maybe it was time I told Maru about our situation—that our parents had married and we'd become siblings. I could explain that was all it was, and that his suspicions were way off the mark.

But what exactly did he suspect?

In the end, though, I used my lack of time as an excuse to cut discussion short and practically fled the scene. In that moment, I lost all right to criticize adults for putting things off and playing it safe to avoid complications.

I dashed into the bookstore without a second to spare. Once inside, I changed into my uniform, put on my apron, and checked my nameplate. Then the moment I stepped out of the changing room, I ran into Ayase and Yomiuri as they did the same.

"Hey, Yuuta!" Yomiuri called out. "Ready for work?"

"Hey, Yomiuri. You bet."

"Hi, Asamura."

"Y-yeah. Hi, Ayase."

I felt a little awkward. I still wasn't over the shock of unexpectedly running into her at the coffee shop.

"It looks like we're the only ones on this shift," Yomiuri noted.

That meant there were just three of us part-timers covering the whole store.

"It sounds like we're a bit understaffed," I said.

"Yeah, but we'll be fine. Saki's worth two of anyone else."

"I wish you wouldn't keep raising your expectations," she said humbly, but Yomiuri was right—her work was outstanding. Ayase was serious and fast. She was always eager to learn new things, and at this point, she was as good at the job as I was.

She really had it together. Her hair might be a flashy shade of blond, but she consistently took out her earrings at work. Although I doubted anyone would judge her by her appearance in this day and age, all sorts of people went to bookstores, so you couldn't be sure what kind of complaints might come in. I didn't think she'd personally care if someone told her off, but she probably didn't want to cause trouble for the business.

She even painted her nails a less noticeable color and refrained from decorating them, since customers would be paying attention to her hands when she worked the register, passing them change or putting covers on books. As long as she did everything perfectly, she wasn't likely to hear any complaints, but she'd had a hard time doing things like removing plastic packaging at first, since she had no previous experience.

It was easy for people to complain when a clumsy newbie was dressed to stand out. I'd never dreamed she would put so much careful effort into avoiding those kinds of risks. She was completely serious about her job, sweating away even in the air-conditioned bookstore.

Us part-timers had to take turns going on break since if we all left at the same time, there would be no one to help serve customers or ring up sales in a pinch.

Ayase took hers around two hours after we started working.

Our breaks weren't long—they only lasted around ten minutes. If we worked a full day, we could take an hour, but on a half-day shift from six to ten PM, we didn't get as much time.

"Okay, I'm going to take a break," Ayase said.

"Sure thing, Saki. Get some rest."

"I'll be back in ten." After confirming, Ayase headed off.

"Hmm..." Yomiuri looked pensive as she watched the other girl walk away.

"What's the matter?" I asked.

There was a regular employee at the register, just ringing up the last customer. People were probably heading out to dinner around now.

Yomiuri flicked her wrist, beckoning me over.

"What is it?" I asked again.

She called me to a spot behind the cash registers and said, "It's about Sakikins."

"What kind of nickname is that?"

"Oh? Do you have a complaint, *Big Brother*?"

"Sometimes, you call her Saki, and then other times, it's Ayase. Talk about being inconsistent."

"Then let's decide on something now. Saki, Saki-poo, Satch… Which is your favorite?"

"Don't ask me. I'm fine with Ayase."

"Then we'll go with Saki."

We'd ended up right back where we started. I didn't care what Yomiuri called her, but I sure hoped she didn't expect me to start using whatever she decided on.

"So what about Ayase?" I asked.

"Tsk!"

"Please don't click your tongue at me."

"This is serious."

"It doesn't seem that way to me."

"I mean your sister. She's way too serious!"

"Oh yeah?"

Was there something wrong with that?

"Oh, don't misunderstand me. She's amazing at her job. She's earnest and hardworking. She's a quick learner, and she makes sure to do everything perfectly. She's a model employee."

"You didn't mention that she's only a part-timer."

"Stop nitpicking! The problem is, she's way too hard on herself when she can't do something."

I gasped.

After prefacing that she was only giving her own opinion, Yomiuri launched into a discussion of Ayase's character.

According to her, Ayase was too ready to blame herself for everything. While that was a trait common among high achievers, Yomiuri was worried Ayase might suffer a nervous breakdown if anything stopped her from progressing or if things suddenly went wrong.

She said she'd known a girl at her college who was a lot like Ayase and that she'd started developing real problems.

"She was a high achiever, too. Apparently, she'd been the best at everything she did since grade school. It wasn't just talent, either. She always worked really hard. But when she got into college, she failed for the first time."

Most people wouldn't think that was anything special.

"Everybody has a few things they can't do no matter how hard they try," she continued. "We're only human, after all. But this girl didn't see it that way. She couldn't forgive herself. She put all the blame on her own shoulders, convincing herself she'd failed because she was lazy."

"So...what happened?"

"She went back home. I think she lived in Shikoku. And after that... I don't know. I hope she's doing well."

It occurred to me that Yomiuri must have been quite the worrier if she was that concerned about a classmate who wasn't even her friend... I kept that thought to myself, however.

According to Yomiuri, people who tended to blame themselves for everything couldn't afford to be sloppy. They couldn't let themselves relax, were always tense, and accumulated stress easily.

In other words, they weren't able to stop by themselves.

Eventually, they'd wear themselves out and become exhausted. If you wanted to stop someone like that—someone who felt they'd die if they didn't keep moving forward—you'd inevitably have to prevent them from doing things they wanted to do. You'd have to go against their free will, precisely because you cared about them.

Yomiuri's explanation reminded me of the time Ayase had lost it and stopped listening to what I was saying. I'd had to force her to stop and listen to me. At the time, I'd been desperate and wasn't fully aware of what I was doing.

It sounded nice to say you always gave things your all, but…

"When you say everything's important, it's kind of like saying nothing is," said Yomiuri. "Don't you agree?"

"So it's 'kind of like' that, but you're not saying it's exactly the same, right?"

"Well, some people really do consider everything important to them. You have to be a prodigy for that, though. Most people are only average. They can only handle so much, and I don't think they need to try to do it all."

"I see. This has been educational."

"So you should save your energy for the things that really count. You have to be a little sloppy. Get it?"

"Yeah. So you're saying we need to remind people like Ayase to take breaks."

"Exactly! That's my Yuuta. So you'll forgive me if I take a slightly longer break than usual, won't you?"

Yomiuri put her palms together in a pleading gesture. She'd already dropped her serious tone and was now casually trying to get a favor out of me.

"What a segue… I suppose there's something you want to do."

"They'll close for the night if I wait till I'm done with my shift. It takes fifteen minutes to get there and come back."

I sighed. Yomiuri was something else…

"All right. You can add my break time to yours. Go ahead and do whatever mystery shopping you want."

"Yes! Gimme a high five."

"Forget it."

"Spoilsport."

"I really can't keep up with you."

I'd been moved by Yomiuri's insights and impressed by her maturity, and now this. What a way to ruin the mood.

"Anyway," she added, "if you truly care about your sister, maybe you should intervene a bit more in her life." And with that, she made her way back toward the registers.

"I need to intervene if I care about her, huh?"

Maybe Yomiuri had been serious, after all. She was just so hard to read.

It was another hot night. I'd finished my shift, and the temperature still hadn't budged.

As I pushed my bicycle alongside Ayase, taking the side closer to the street, I thought back to what Yomiuri had said.

Ayase had been making a big effort at work for the past month. I figured it was all so she could bulk up her savings in the hopes of moving out on her own. It was partly my fault for not being able to track down a job where she could make quick money—instead, she'd chosen to become my coworker so she could learn the ropes from someone she knew. All that made sense.

But just as Dad had said, I hadn't seen her enjoying herself even once during that time. Something Maru had mentioned was also nagging at me.

"We need to remind people like Ayase to take breaks."

Hmm. Maybe I should ask her about it…

"Hey, Ayase? Is there any chance that Narasaka invited you to go to the pool? …And maybe me, too?"

"…Has Maaya contacted you?" she asked immediately, frowning. *So it's true.*

"Nope. Narasaka doesn't have my contact details."

"Then how do you know about it?" She was clearly suspicious.

"Someone told me—that's all. I had no idea."

I explained that I'd heard from a friend that Narasaka was planning a get-together at a swimming pool.

"Do you want to go?" she asked.

For a minute, I thought she was asking if I wanted to go *with her*. Then I realized she was only asking if I was interested in going to the pool.

Ayase didn't like to leave room for misunderstanding, so when she asked a question like that, there was never any hidden meaning behind her words. She was simply asking if I wanted to go. In that case, I should tell her exactly what I thought.

"To be honest, I think I'd just stand out if I went to a pool with a bunch of extroverts. So no, I'm not crazy about the idea." I could tell I had a wry smile on my face as I answered.

For a moment, I thought I saw a lonely look cross Ayase's face as we passed under a streetlight.

"No? Then you don't need to force yourself."

Her curt reply bothered me. I couldn't tell what feeling was behind it. It might have been anger or even sadness. In a strange way, I also sensed a kind of relief.

"Aren't you going?" I asked. "To the pool, I mean."

"No, I'm not."

"Why not?"

"……"

When I decided to press her further, she clammed up. Cars were continuously zooming down the road to my side, so perhaps she simply hadn't heard me. But if she had, it might annoy her if I kept pushing.

I was left with a strange uneasiness.

"No, I'm not."

I wondered what she was feeling when she said that.

As we kept walking, the lights of our building blinked into view down the road. I had to park my bike, so I told her to go ahead. Once alone, I continued to think about her right up until I opened the door to our apartment.

● AUGUST 24 (MONDAY)

That morning, I woke up and went into the living room, only to find no one there.

I knew Dad and Akiko were out. Dad had already left for work, and Akiko hadn't come home yet. She had contacted us saying she'd be late (or early, in this case).

But Ayase was missing, too, and she was usually up at this hour. Was she in her room? But it wasn't that hot in the living room. In fact, it was nice and cool.

Huh? Cool?

Just then, I realized something strange.

Cool air was coming out of the air conditioner. It was fixed. I'd come home late last night and gone straight to my room without eating dinner, so I hadn't noticed. It seemed a repairman had come during the day and worked on it. I remembered Dad and Akiko saying they were going shopping, but maybe they'd prioritized the repairs.

They must've left it on for me, knowing I'd be up soon.

I glanced toward the dining room and saw breakfast sitting on the table.

Could it be? I checked my phone and saw a text message from Ayase.

I made breakfast, so dig in. I already ate.

That meant she was up. She must be in her room, studying or cleaning.

I sent her a thank-you and took my usual seat at the table.

"So it's a traditional Japanese breakfast today."

Grilled salmon was on the blue plate used for fish, with a small mound of grated daikon radish and two tiny pickled plums near the edge. Another plate held a pack of seaweed for seasoning, and another bigger plate held a salad. It reminded me of the kinds of breakfasts you got at traditional Japanese inns.

As always, I sent Ayase my silent thanks.

After I'd glanced over everything, I picked up the empty rice and miso soup bowls Ayase had set on the table, stood up, and headed into the kitchen. There, I reheated the soup, filling my rice bowl from the cooker in the meantime. Before the soup came to a boil, I turned off the stove, filled my soup bowl, and returned to the table.

I folded my hands and said my thanks for the meal, then began eating.

After pouring soy sauce over the grated daikon and letting it soak in, I scooped it up and placed it on the salmon. Then, using my chopsticks to break the salmon into pieces, I ate it all together.

The sweetness of the fish, mixed with the sharp flavor of the daikon, spread through my mouth with every bite.

Fish is so good. It was delicious in a different way from other meat. The grated daikon left a refreshing aftertaste that guaranteed I'd be able to follow it up with a bunch of rice.

I love a good, simple Japanese meal, I thought as I reached for the miso soup. It was a pretty cliché sentiment, but it was true.

That morning, the soup contained tiny *nameko* mushrooms. I savored their slippery texture, coated in miso paste, as I chewed and swallowed them down along with the soup.

Once again, Ayase's work was a triumph.

I always felt like sending her my thoughts via text, but I was too afraid it'd seem creepy if I messaged her about something so trivial. It was different when I could tell her in person.

Instead, I sent her my thoughts and appreciation silently in my heart.

Thank you for always making such delicious miso soup, Ayase.

After I finished eating and cleaning up, I still had a little time before I needed to leave for work. Wondering what to do, I glanced around the living room and decided to help out with the cleaning.

I covered the rest of the food on the table with plastic wrap to protect it from dust. I could have put it away in the refrigerator, but Akiko would be home soon, and I thought it would be better not to cool the grilled fish too much. If she decided not to eat, I'd put it away.

A good rule of thumb for housecleaning was to work from the top down, since dust would keep falling toward the floor. I wiped the surfaces I could reach, gave the floor a rough sweep, and then used a mop to polish the wood. Cleaning kept my hands busy, but my mind began to wander. I started thinking about how strangely Ayase had been acting over the last few days.

It had started on Saturday.

"Don't worry about Maaya. We aren't the type of friends who go out together during summer break, okay?"

I couldn't figure out why she'd come all the way to my room just to tell me something like that. Would Ayase really do something so irrational?

"Hmm."

I stopped moving the mop, rested my chin on its handle, and groaned.

That was when I remembered something else.

Maru had said that I was also invited to Narasaka's pool party, but no one had contacted me. Nobody in Narasaka's group had my contact info, of course, so that made sense. They couldn't invite me even if they wanted to.

In that case, what was Narasaka to do? She'd probably ask Ayase to invite me.

It made sense for Ayase to refuse if she didn't want to go, but it *didn't* make sense for her to purposely not tell me about it.

I thought about what I would do in her position. What if Maru made a similar plan and asked me to invite Ayase along? Even if I wasn't going, I'd definitely tell her about it. I'd say, "Maru invited you to come do such and such with us."

If I didn't, my selfish decision would be robbing her of a potentially fun outing. Our relationship was supposed to be fair and equal, and something like that just wouldn't sit right with me.

So why hadn't she told me? Something was off. As I thought this, I realized I'd stopped cleaning altogether.

"Oops!"

I resumed working on the living room, though my mind was still occupied with thoughts of Ayase and what she was up to. I had just finished polishing the floor when I heard the front door open and saw Akiko stagger into the room like she was ready to crash.

"Oh…Yuuta. G'mornin'."

"Welcome home, and good morning. Would you like something to eat?"

"Yeah… I'll just have some ice cream and go to bed," she said, her eyes half closed.

I opened the freezer compartment of our fridge, took out an ice cream bar (Dad had made sure we were fully stocked with a whole selection of the stuff since Akiko loved it), and offered it to her. It was strawberry flavored.

"Oh, by the way," I said, "did you guys have the air conditioner fixed yesterday?"

"Mm… Oh yeah, we did. Taichi called the repairman right away, so…"

She seemed really tired, and her sentences kept trailing off.

She sat down and started into her ice cream while she explained. Apparently, the air conditioner's filter had been dirty. Dad had tried to fix it on his own and almost caused even more problems. But fortunately, the repairman had seen to it.

Dad had probably been trying to show off in front of Akiko. What a mess.

"Machines are so complicated, aren't they?" Akiko mused. "They seem perfectly fine, and then one day, they suddenly break down."

My heart skipped a beat.

They seem perfectly fine—until they suddenly break down. In my mind, her words became linked to what Yomiuri had said the other day about serious people abruptly suffering a nervous breakdown.

Maybe it wasn't just machines. Maybe the same thing was true of people.

Serious people couldn't stop by themselves. If you didn't force them to rest, they'd break down one day. But how would Ayase take a suggestion like that?

"Does Ayase dislike people who try to force her to stop doing what she wants to do?"

I put the question to Akiko, hoping to get a handle on Ayase's personality before I made my move. Akiko stopped eating her ice cream, stared into space, and thought about it.

"Hmm? Are you asking if she dislikes people pushing her to do things?"

"P-pushing her…?" I supposed you could put it that way, though the nuance seemed a little different. "Not necessarily pushing her, I guess. I mean, uh, for example, if someone made plans and then tried to get her to come along. Something like that."

"So you're asking if she likes people pressuring her to go on dates? Well, knowing her, I don't think she'd be very happy about it. I think most girls prefer their partner to go through all the proper steps."

"So she wouldn't like it… I kind of figured."

Akiko's take on her daughter's personality sounded pretty accurate. *But then what should I do to get her to relax…?*

"Hmm?" Akiko suddenly cut into my thoughts. "Do you want to ask her out on a date? Yuuta…have you fallen in love with her?"

I froze. *What was that? Um, what did she ask me just now?* Panicking, I went back over our exchange in my mind. Could I have caused a misunderstanding?

"N-no!" I exclaimed. "That's not what I meant. I wasn't talking about a romantic relationship. I just thought Ayase might be taking things too seriously."

I needed to explain myself. Very carefully, I went over what Yomiuri and I had discussed the previous day.

Akiko smiled; she looked convinced. It appeared she'd understood me. I sighed in relief.

"Now I get it," she said. "For a minute there, I wondered if you might have fallen for her."

"I would never—"

That wasn't possible.

Ayase was my younger sister. My *sister.* I couldn't fall for her. That just wasn't possible.

"Yes, well. I think you might be right about Saki," Akiko muttered, bringing me out of my thoughts. "I became very busy around the time she started junior high. And Saki, in turn, tried to help me out by putting as little of a burden on me as she could. She became very independent—too independent for a girl her age."

"Yeah... That's how it looks to me, too."

"Yes. It may sound like a good thing, but when I think about how it's all my fault for not being able to take care of her properly...I regret that. I feel like I took advantage of her. I wish I could have allowed her to stay a carefree child a little longer."

I wish I could have allowed her to stay a carefree child a little longer.

Akiko's words broke my heart. I thought back to the photo I'd seen of Ayase as a young girl—a girl who used to ask her mom for ice cream and begged to go to the pool. But Ayase forced herself to grow up. She decided to live independently without relying on anyone.

It began with her desire to ease the burden on her mom. But now it was more than that.

"Yuuta," Akiko said, and I glanced up at her. She was staring at me with a serious look in her eyes. "I really shouldn't ask this of my stepson, but would you help Saki take a breather now and then so she doesn't work too hard? If she pushes back, then you can use a little force, as you mentioned."

I hesitated for a moment, then nodded.

Up until now, I'd tried to maintain a certain distance from other people. I couldn't and didn't want to be responsible for their lives, and I didn't like having others barge into my own business, either. I tried to avoid relationships of mutual dependence, where I and someone else would become a burden on each other.

I recalled what Ayase had said when we first met:

"I won't expect anything from you, and I don't want you to expect anything from me."

That was why I'd found her words back then such a relief. I thought that, if possible, it would be best to keep our relationship relaxed and relatively distant.

But if she was hurtling toward a breakdown, I couldn't simply sit back and watch.

Not even if it meant she would hate me.

"Don't worry. If she starts hating you, I'll tell you the thing she likes best."

"The thing she likes best... Hmm. Will that, uh, make her happy again?"

"Absolutely!" Akiko broke into a grin.

She had a nice smile. Though I was skeptical such a convenient remedy really existed, I asked Akiko to tell me about it if the time came.

I didn't want Ayase to hate me.

She was my little sister, after all, and we still shared a roof.

The only sound in the living room was the quiet hum of the air conditioner.

After thanking me for the ice cream, Akiko tossed the stick into the trash. She must have been really tired. She staggered away, her body swaying, as she proceeded to her and Dad's bedroom. I was a little worried whether she would make it into bed without keeling over. *Good job at work, and good night. Now, then...*

I put the uneaten grilled salmon in the fridge and went to knock on Ayase's door.

"What is it?"

I could see a narrow cutout of her desk through the gap in the door. A notebook and textbook lay open, and she was holding a pair of headphones in her hand. She must have just taken them off. Instead of earbuds, she was using those heavy-duty headphones that covered your entire ear. I guessed she was listening to lofi hip-hop while she studied. The air conditioner in her room was on full blast, and it was a little cooler than the living room. Akiko had said earlier that Ayase didn't like hot weather.

"Hey, about Narasaka's pool party—"

"I'm not going," she said bluntly, not waiting for me to finish. When she saw me clam up awkwardly, she added, almost like an excuse, "I don't have the time to let loose at some pool."

That's exactly the problem, I thought.

I knew she wasn't trying to irritate me. Making time to play was *running away* in her book. She didn't believe it was necessary to "let loose" sometimes. To use an old Japanese expression, she reminded me of someone with a heart as straight as young green bamboo.

I thought over my next move. If I kept pushing, she'd only grow more and more intractable. I took a breath, then continued:

"Okay, that's fine. But I've been thinking about going. So, uh, will you give me Narasaka's contact information?"

My plan was to make a show of having fun in front of Ayase, then get her to loosen up a little, too. She turned back to me and looked me right in the eye.

"No."

"Huh? Uh…"

Her response caught me by surprise. I hadn't expected her to refuse outright.

Ayase disliked reactions that were illogical and based only on emotion, so I didn't think she would turn me down. Narasaka had been trying to reach me, after all.

Ayase looked like she'd surprised herself a bit.

"Uh, I mean, it's not polite to give someone another person's contact information…," she said at last.

"Oh…"

So that was it. She was right. In that case, her refusal *was* logical. Personal information had to be protected. You could count on Ayase to be mindful of all the little details.

At that point, I fully believed her.

"I'll ask Maaya," she said, "and let you know once she replies, okay?"

"Got it."

She would probably send Narasaka a text or an e-mail, which wouldn't take long. She said she had to study, so I let her go. I'd see her at work that evening anyway. I closed her door and returned to my room.

I wasn't so concerned about whether I could drag her to the pool or not. She saw her schoolwork and her part-time job as an immovable mountain towering before her. As long as she felt that way, she'd have a huge amount of psychological pressure.

Going to the pool wasn't important. My only concern was that she let herself relax before she broke down.

I figured I'd talk to her again at work.

That afternoon, I left our apartment.

I rode my bike through blasts of suffocatingly hot air as they rose off the concrete below. My route took me down an uneven, hilly road, past several train stations. To cope with the heat, I'd slipped a bottle of mineral water in my bike's basket along with my bag, where it was easy to reach.

I felt sweat pouring out under my clothes and grimaced, but it didn't change the fact that I enjoyed my commute.

As I pedaled through the Omotesando area, which was currently full of college students on summer break, I saw one building that looked a cut above all the others. It was a famous prep school that exhorted its students to try for the prestigious University of Tokyo.

As I parked my bike and stepped into the building, I felt strangely relaxed. This place, with its serious air, suited me better than the partygoing atmosphere of Shibuya or the rest of the Omotesando area. Outside the prep school, you could find a lot of popular boutiques, and female college students were lining up in front of a pancake house that was perfect for taking selfies to share on social media.

I went into a classroom inside the school and secured a desk as close to the corner as possible. Unlike high school, you could sit wherever you wanted, but it seemed like human nature to keep using the same desk as long as it was available.

Incidentally, I wasn't a regular student at the prep school. I was only attending a summer class.

Most of the other students appeared to be here for the same purpose, and no one was chatting away, like you might at a regular school. Everyone had their textbooks open as they quietly focused on their work.

My school, Suisei High, was also an elite institution, but its students weren't all like this. Perhaps the difference in the atmosphere—whether it was serious or relaxed—came down to interpersonal relationships, rather than grades or personality.

All the students here had black hair, as opposed to hair dyed brown or blond. No one wore flashy jewelry or makeup, and everyone's shirts were buttoned up properly. Most of them were what society at large viewed as the solemn, studious type. The sharp way they stared at their textbooks was totally different from my classmates at Suisei.

They were all like Ayase, I thought all of a sudden.

Appearance-wise, they were totally different, but the way they bent over their textbooks and the earnestness in their eyes was similar.

They were all giving this 100 percent. They looked like soldiers about to go to war.

They weren't like me—only interested in getting into as decent a college as I could manage on my own merit.

But I got the feeling that, even compared with the people here, Ayase had an especially bad habit of overextending herself. Not only was she aiming to become economically independent, but she was also doing everything by herself, without joining any expensive summer classes. If any other high schooler had declared they were going to do it all on their own, people would probably tease them and say they were just being contrary. But Ayase had managed to get high marks in every subject. Nobody could tease her.

Over the past month, she'd even managed to mostly overcome her weakness—Modern Japanese. Every day, she was becoming more of a model candidate for university.

As for me…I wasn't as dedicated to hard work. I figured I'd take in what I could from my summer classes and gradually improve my abilities. It was important to know your own limitations.

"U-um…"

"Huh? Oh, did you need something?"

It took me a moment to respond to the faint voice. It was the first time someone had approached me during a summer class, and at first, I didn't realize that she was talking to me.

It was the girl who sat next to me. She didn't always take the same seat, but I'd seen her sit nearby on several occasions. She didn't have a wild hairstyle or eccentric fashion, but one thing *did* stand out about her: her height.

She was probably around a hundred and eighty centimeters—a head taller than I was, and I felt oddly intimidated with her standing in front of me.

"You dropped something," she said. For her height, she had an unexpectedly insecure-sounding voice.

"O-oh, I did?"

I recognized the bookmark on the floor. I must have dropped it when I opened my textbook.

"Th-thank you," I said as I picked it up, and our eyes met. She'd been staring at the bookmark.

"That's from the summer fair. It's the one they're handing out at the bookstore by the train station, isn't it?"

"Oh, um, yes."

I couldn't tell her that I worked there. It wasn't smart to give your personal information out to strangers.

"What a coincidence. I often pass by that store."

"I think most people living in this area buy their books there."

"That's true. Ah-ha-ha." The tall girl laughed lightheartedly.

That was the end of our conversation. She hadn't wanted to talk to me in particular. She was being nice, telling me that I'd dropped something, and we happened to have a topic—the bookstore—in common. It was just an everyday exchange with no particular meaning.

I glanced at her profile as she took her seat and felt a little uncomfortable.

...Had I seen a customer like her at the store?

She probably kept similar hours to me, since we were both high school students, but I didn't recall catching sight of her at the cash register. I was sure I'd remember a girl of her stature—she was like a model.

But I didn't work twenty-four seven, and she probably didn't come to the store that frequently. Plus, it wasn't unheard of for two people to be in the same place and miss each other. I kept telling myself that as I turned my focus back to my studies.

My class that day was otherwise completely ordinary. I had no more exchanges with the girl, and time went by as usual. I concentrated on my studies from afternoon until evening.

Once our last section was over, I checked the time and saw I had about forty minutes until my late shift began. The bookstore was about ten minutes away by bike. Naturally, I had considered that when I chose this prep school.

I put my books in my bag and briskly walked out of the building toward the parking area. There, I unlocked my bike and got on. I'd been doing the same thing all summer, and it was basically routine by now. I barely had to think.

But then something different happened.

"Huh?" I blinked.

As I began pedaling my bike in a daze, I caught sight of someone familiar sitting at one of the outdoor tables in front of that popular pancake house right next to my prep school.

Her long black hair was fixed in place with a fancy hairband, and she wore a top made of soft fabric that gently hugged her skin, along with a flared skirt. This woman dressed like some trim noble girl was none other than my coworker, Shiori Yomiuri.

Was she with her college friends? She sat at a table for four with three other women, and they appeared to be having a serious discussion as they elegantly sliced into their pancakes.

Because of our proximity and the fact that they were talking fairly loudly, I could hear what they were saying.

Two of the women looked to be college girls around Yomiuri's age, but the other was clearly different—she had a dignified, mature air about her.

While the students wore light summer clothes, the older woman, who seemed like something of an intellectual, had on a long-sleeved cardigan despite the heat. She kept looking from one girl to another as if she was assessing them.

"Okay then, can anyone offer a counterargument? When people compare the humanities we study to the natural sciences, they call them 'soft sciences' that don't contribute to society and question their value. If you can't convince them otherwise, you won't be able to justify your research."

Perhaps intimidated, the girls glanced at one another solemnly and hesitated.

The intellectual woman maintained a confident smile as she elegantly sliced her pancake and carried a bite to her mouth.

Their discussion certainly wasn't what you'd expect to hear at a trendy pancake house. But perhaps the other patrons found it so incomprehensible that it didn't bother them. Whatever the reason, Yomiuri's group fit surprisingly well into the surrounding scene.

Despite the strange mood at the table, one of the girls bravely spoke up—it was Yomiuri.

"If we define the natural sciences as the pursuit of identifying reproducible laws through experimentation, then in terms of technological advancement and contribution to human society, they are indeed superior. As long as that's true, I don't believe we can form a counterargument based on a denial of that fact."

"That's very wise. You seem to understand that twisting the truth for the sake of refutation is a bad idea."

"Yes. And yet, despite that, humanities are still a valuable pursuit."

"How? The study of literature and historical fact is just for fun. How do you justify devoting the nation's precious research resources to such useless studies?"

"Unraveling the history of our ancestors is essential to answering the fundamental question of how human beings should live their lives."

"Do you really think so? Literature and history are merely records of the past left by certain individuals. Understanding them won't help us grasp general tendencies among humans as a species."

"By learning about the past, we can understand the future. We can also look to the past for clues on how to solve modern problems."

"You're saying history repeats itself?"

"Yes, exactly. All social strife is rooted in causes that have arisen numerous times in the past. I believe that by studying the past, we can find appropriate answers to our present problems."

"Come now, Yomiuri. That's a bit of a stretch."

"Huh?"

"The adage that history repeats itself is nothing but the opinion of those with a past. No amount of historical research into a past with virtually no quantitative data can prove the repeatability of events."

"Ngh…!"

Yomiuri was at a loss for words. It seemed the older woman had hit a sore spot.

Rudely twirling her knife next to her head, she continued: "Today, it has become possible to look at all kinds of phenomena through the lens of data. The ease with which it can be acquired and collected brings to light previously unprovable human truths. People in the future may have much to learn from the past, but that past is our present. If we want to learn from the past to solve future problems, we should first focus on the achievements of the natural sciences. Okay, any counterarguments?"

The woman jerked her chin, and Yomiuri immediately responded:

"The values of modern people are based on a continuous cultural tradition. By understanding literature, history, religion, and other customs, we can correctly comprehend how we arrived at where we are today. For example, if an artist from one country makes a music video that disrespects another country's religion, resulting in a huge public outcry, is there any way to use the natural sciences to figure out what caused that reaction? Can they be used to predict and draft a plan to settle the issue? A humanities researcher could immediately formulate a number of hypotheses."

"Hmm. That's quite an aggressive rebuttal but not a bad line of reasoning."

It must have been a good argument. The older woman stopped moving her knife and appeared to mull over what Yomiuri had said for a few seconds.

But a few seconds were all it took. She was soon speaking again.

"How do you prove cause and effect if the cause of the anger is rooted in the country's unique history and religion?"

"What?!"

"Did the anger really occur because the group's culture was disrespected? Perhaps the sounds used in the video were simply offensive to the human brain. Or maybe the colors amplified their rage."

"It should be possible to produce some correlation through social experiments and questionnaires given to the involved parties."

"Okay, I think we're done."

"Huh? ...Oh!"

With a smile on her face, the older woman stole a piece of pancake from the plate in front of Yomiuri, who sat there stunned. She then bit into the pancake with innocent gusto, completely at odds with her intellectual appearance.

"Unfortunately, I can't support your view," she said. "You just admitted that it's meaningless to pore over past literature and that research on what is happening today is more important. Too bad. You'll have to work harder on your quibbling."

"Ngh...!"

Done in, Yomiuri held her head in frustration. Using her fork, she stabbed the remaining piece of pancake on her plate and shoved it into her mouth. I was truly astonished by the childlike way her cheeks puffed out as she chewed.

Her exchanges with the older woman, the way she looked—I was seeing a completely different Yomiuri from the one I knew at the bookstore. She always seemed so confident in front of me that it was kind of refreshing.

She turned to the older woman and asked, "Professor Kudou, how can you speak so eloquently in the negative? Don't you belong to the faculty of humanities?"

So the intellectual-looking woman was named Kudou. She must have been a professor or maybe an associate professor. I'd read somewhere that you had to be fairly old to become a professor, and this woman still looked young.

"Easy. I understand the difference between what one thinks and what one says."

"I see… Then what would be *your* argument?"

"I'd start by saying, 'What's wrong with being a soft science?'"

"…Huh?"

"While the humanities are often defined as soft sciences, there is room for argument against the preconception that such endeavors can't contribute to humanity. Our adversaries say developments in the natural sciences will surely result in people's happiness, but you must first define *people's happiness* for that to have any meaning. Unfortunately, there is no common definition of concepts like justice or happiness among humans. For example, I am utterly delighted eating sweet pancakes as I am now doing, but I wonder what percentage of humanity would agree."

"Isn't happiness from a biological standpoint defined by the ability to leave offspring?"

"Are you saying people who can't have children are unhappy?"

"…I see your point. And in this day and age, not many people feel that way."

"Exactly. In the end, concepts like what constitutes happiness for humanity, or how humans ought to live their lives, are extremely hard to pin down. Developments brought about by the natural sciences are necessarily built atop that shaky foundation. The practical sciences only exist because of the soft sciences, and denying them will bring us all crashing down together. So if you don't want that, accept us! …That's my answer anyway."

"Oh… I see. Okay…"

"It was a good idea to call attention to the subject of communication with other countries. You might have had more success if you first accepted the soft sciences on their own merits before trying to affirm them."

"This has been very educational… Thank you, Professor," Yomiuri said with a bow. Then she sighed deeply. "*Haah*… I can't get anywhere in an argument."

"No, you were great, Yomiuri," said one of the other girls. "I couldn't keep up from the very start."

"Me neither."

"Hey," the professor cut in, "don't think you all are off the hook. I'm treating you to these expensive pancakes, and I expect you to use your brains to make it worth my while. Okay, let's move on to our next topic—"

The girls let out what sounded like a tiny scream. "Are you kidding?! If Yomiuri can't win an argument against you, there's zero hope for us!"

As the discussion shifted to the next subject, Yomiuri looked away from the other girls, perhaps to hide her frustration.

That was when, by sheer coincidence—or perhaps it was inevitable, considering our positions—her eyes met mine where I sat atop my bicycle.

Crap.

I'd started listening in by pure chance, but when you stopped to think about it, I'd clearly been eavesdropping. It was not very polite behavior on my part.

But Yomiuri quickly looked away, glanced at her watch, and said, "Oh!" in a very exaggerated manner. "I'm sorry, Professor, I have to go to work."

"Yes, go ahead. Don't worry about the check."

"Thank you."

She bowed politely, swung her bag over her shoulder, and dashed away.

She shot me a look as she passed by, which I took as a silent message. I started pedaling my bike, following her.

Several minutes went by as I proceeded along Cat Street. Once we were too far to be seen from the pancake house, I approached her from behind.

"Sorry," I said.

"You're apologizing? Does that mean you acknowledge your crime?"

"It's all a misunderstanding. I just happened to be passing by."

"I can't decide if you're too stubborn or not stubborn enough. Either way, you're definitely guilty. But…I know you weren't stalking me."

"I'm thrilled to hear you trust me."

"You're too smart for that. If you really wanted to stalk someone, you'd be a lot creepier about it."

"That isn't the type of trust I wanted…" To clear up her suspicions, I opened my bag and showed her my textbook. "I'm taking summer classes. My prep school is over there."

"Oh. Roger that."

"Ten-four. Are we all square?"

"I see now. So you just happened to be there, and you just happened to eavesdrop."

"I..."

She'd set me up.

Like some master detective, she'd used clever questioning to corner me into a confession. I was at a loss for words, and she burst out laughing.

"Just kidding. I was only getting back at you for witnessing me embarrass myself. Okay, let's go!"

"Oh, right!"

I hopped off my bike and pushed it along as I followed Yomiuri. Once I caught up, I glanced over at her.

Her beautiful black hair swayed with each elegant gesture, and she wore a clean, trim outfit. Illuminated by the bright sunlight, she looked more and more like some rich family's pampered daughter. During summer, the evenings were as bright as day. When we'd gone to see a movie all that time ago, it had been dark outside, and I hadn't noticed it. But seeing her in her regular clothes now under the light, the impression was even more powerful.

"Ugh, I can't believe you saw me clenching my fists over losing an argument. My dignity as your senior has been damaged."

"Oh, I wouldn't say that..."

That would imply you had dignity to begin with, I thought. I'd almost said it out loud, and I had a feeling she'd caught my drift. She was glaring at me. I quickly changed the subject, not wanting to further invoke her wrath.

"Who was that woman you were with?" I asked.

"You mean Professor Kudou?"

"Yes, her."

"You sure are a bore as a guy. Three college girls were sitting at that table, and yet you're more interested in the older woman."

"Isn't it rude to talk about a woman's age?"

"Women are allowed to as a special case, Yuuta."

Are you imitating her now? Yomiuri would probably sulk if I said that, so I kept my mouth shut. I'd just be causing more trouble for myself otherwise.

"Kudou is an associate professor at our college. You probably guessed that, judging by her age."

"Yeah, pretty much. But it's summer break. Does she often go to pancake houses with students like that?"

"She sometimes invites us, although not many students go."

"But as an intellectual, you're different."

"Hmm, I don't like how you said that. I'll give you fifty out of a hundred."

"Don't tell me you can't handle it. You tease me the same way all the time."

"I'm an intellectu*elle*. I'm a girl, you know."

"Oh."

She didn't appear to mind being called an intellectual.

"Maybe you can't tell from the way I usually talk to you, but I *am* one of the more serious students at my college."

"I know you're smart, so I'm not all that surprised… But like they say, there's always a bigger fish."

"Kudou *is* a little otherworldly."

"I wouldn't know. I only saw her talking with you for a few moments."

"She's always like that. She's unfathomable, and I often can't tell what she's thinking."

"That's what you're like to me."

To me, Yomiuri was an unreadable older woman. I had no idea what was going on in her mind. Her vast stores of knowledge and the way she could call it all up at the drop of a hat were simply beyond me. I often felt like she had me wrapped around her little finger. Maybe that was just the generation gap. I wondered: If I was somehow able to get on her level, would I start to understand the meaning behind her words and actions?

As I mulled this over, Yomiuri frowned. "Come on—cut it out."

"What are you talking about?"

"You must be thinking about how you can surpass me."

"Huh?" Unable to figure out how she'd jumped to such a conclusion, I let out an embarrassing squeal.

"You're frustrated by your lack of knowledge and wisdom, and you've just vowed to one-up me someday."

"I didn't know education was so competitive."

"That's my way of enjoying it. Surprised?"

"No. Actually, I agree."

Judging strictly by appearances, Yomiuri seemed like the kind of girl who took her studies seriously and had a genuine love of reading. However, she had a habit of bringing a childish sense of rivalry to the table that reminded me more of a grade schooler. But that was Shiori Yomiuri for you.

"That said, intense discussions like the one you were having earlier sound exhausting."

"Well, sure they are. You have to stay on your toes and make sure there aren't any holes in your logic. There's no room to relax. Kudou always jumps right in if you say something inconsistent. I don't like having those discussions before work. They really take it out of me, mentally *and* physically."

"You looked pretty enthusiastic to me."

"If I'm going to do it, I have to give it my all, even if it's a hassle. But… it's fine. I've already recovered."

"What do you mean?"

"I maintain good mental health by teasing you. Talking to you is sooo relaxing."

"It sounds like you just enjoy sniping newbies."

"You're like a nice, comfy armchair, young man," she said, mimicking an elderly woman. She then pretended to lose her balance and placed her hand on my bicycle's basket.

"Um."

I started to tell her not to treat me like an armchair, but I suddenly stopped myself.

I'd just realized something—*this* was the big difference between Yomiuri and Ayase.

We left Cat Street, and the main road came into view. Our bookstore was right up ahead. I'd ended up walking with Yomiuri instead of riding my bike.

Yomiuri probably accepted Kudou's invitations whenever she asked her out, regardless of how troublesome it was or how bad the timing. She considered it advantageous to go, so she did, but she couldn't avoid the resulting physical and mental exhaustion.

Despite all that, Yomiuri maintained a kind of balance. She knew how to even it all out. She knew she could tease me to a certain extent, and I'd put up with it. Even if her arguments weren't sound, we were just having fun, so no one would call her out on it. By enjoying herself that way, she could strike a balance between her serious side and her not-so-serious side.

I wondered if Ayase's problems could be resolved if she had someone like that around.

"Oh…" As I was entertaining these thoughts, Yomiuri and I stepped into the store and ran straight into Ayase. The day had been full of coincidences, but I supposed this wasn't that unexpected since we were all on the same shift.

"Hey, Saki!"

"Mm… Um, hey there. So the two of you came together today."

Our encounter must have also caught Ayase by surprise. For just a moment, she wore the same cool look I always saw her make at home, before she quickly pasted on a friendly smile. Yomiuri alone looked totally carefree.

"We happened to spot each other near his prep school. Right, Yuuta?"

"Uh… Right."

It took me a moment to respond.

Maybe because I'd been thinking of Ayase just then, I felt a bit awkward, even though I hadn't done anything wrong.

"You just happened to spot each other, huh?" Ayase said. She seemed to be tasting each word as she said it. Then she flashed us a broad grin. "As his sister, I'm relieved he's found a wonderful person like you."

"Oh? Aren't you a tease, Saki?"

"It's all thanks to your coaching. Heh-heh!" Ayase laughed softly,

bobbing her shoulders up and down. She had impressive adaptability—she was already mastering conversations with Yomiuri.

Still, something seemed strange.

Had I ever seen her tease someone based on an unconfirmed assumption before?

I had a lot of questions—about, among other things, the weird way she was acting and about going to the pool. I tried to approach her during work, but unfortunately, the timing just never seemed to work out.

When we stood next to each other at the register, every time I was free, she would be ringing up sales. When I was folding book covers, she would walk away to clean up the shelves. I finally asked her during my break if she had heard back from Narasaka, but all she did was shake her head slightly before stepping out of the store, saying she wanted to go buy a drink.

I was starting to think she was avoiding me.

Eventually, it was time to go home. I got ready to leave and stood around, waiting for Ayase.

But the only one who came out of the women's changing room was Yomiuri.

"Oh, I have a message for you, Yuuta," she said. "Saki already left. She said she wanted to stop by someplace on her way home."

"Huh?"

I blinked. Ayase hadn't said anything like that to me. I quickly pulled out my cell phone and checked my messages, only to find she hadn't sent me a single one. I was still standing in a daze when my phone started vibrating. Realizing something was incoming, I looked at it and saw a message flash across the screen.

I'm going shopping, so don't wait up for me.

I opened up my text app to see the entire message, but there wasn't any more to it.

Got it, I replied.

It was true that some shops stayed open after ten. Maybe she was buying something private and wasn't comfortable with me tagging along. Still, the suddenness of it felt odd.

I wondered again if she was avoiding me. *Nah. Why would she do that?*

I rode my bicycle home, and before I knew it, I was standing in front of our apartment building. It hit me then how quickly I could get home on my bike. But when I asked myself if that mattered to me, I found that it didn't.

At some point, I'd gotten used to walking home with Ayase.

I parked my bike in the apartment lot, got on the elevator, and headed for our floor.

It was Monday, so Dad was probably home and in bed since he had to get up early the next morning. Akiko was likely at work.

I whispered, "I'm home," so I wouldn't wake Dad, then headed for the living room.

Normally, I'd come home with Ayase, and she would make dinner... but I couldn't keep depending on her. *Okay, let's do it.* I opened the refrigerator and found a salad and a pot covered with plastic wrap.

"Looks like miso soup."

Since it was summer, Ayase threw anything premade into the fridge or the freezer.

I figured she'd be home soon, so I opened up the cupboard and took out two sets of bowls for rice and soup, then set the table. I could fill them later. I brought out the salad, then checked the refrigerator and freezer again, wondering what the main dish was. In the freezer, I found a number of small plastic containers.

"What are these?"

I pulled them out and saw that they contained rice that'd been cooked with various ingredients and frozen. The rice was colored brown from the dashi soup stock and was mixed in with thinly sliced shiitake mushrooms, carrots, and fried bean curd.

"I'm home."

I turned around and saw Ayase coming through the door into the apartment.

"What's the matter? Oh, dinner... Sorry, I'll get it ready right away."

"Oh, no, you always take care of it. I thought I'd handle it for once. What am I supposed to do with this?" I pointed to the rice in the plastic containers.

Having never cooked rice in my life, it hadn't once occurred to me to make a large batch and freeze it. I wondered if she'd been doing this for a while. I'd watched her going back and forth between the refrigerator and the microwave but hadn't given any thought to what exactly she'd been doing.

"Oh, that. I made it ahead of time today. All you have to do is pop it in the microwave."

"...How many minutes?"

"It's written right there on the machine."

What she said didn't click, so I went over to the device and looked. Next to the timer, there were several buttons with pictures of foods on them.

"Oh, this."

I found a picture of a bowl of rice with the word *reheat* next to it. I'd been using the microwave for five years, and I had never noticed it before.

I placed two of the frozen packages inside and was about to hit start when Ayase stopped me.

"Wait. Remove the lid."

I looked at the square, shallow containers. Puzzled, I tilted my head.

"If you leave the rice covered, it gets sticky and gross from the ice melting."

"I...see."

I didn't understand what she was saying, but if it resulted in tastier rice, then it was probably wiser to follow her instructions. Ayase heated the miso soup I'd taken out of the fridge while I microwaved the rice.

Dinner consisted of rice mixed with shiitake mushrooms and other ingredients, miso soup with tofu, and salad. Ayase took some cherry tomatoes out of the fridge, sliced them into fourths, and placed them on the salad. The salad had lettuce, cabbage, and thin strips of daikon radish. The tomatoes added red to the green and white and made it look fancy.

"That final touch makes it look especially delicious," I noted.

"Japanese dishes you make at home tend to be brownish, so throwing in tomatoes or red and yellow bell peppers is a nice addition."

Bell peppers were usually green, but I'd started seeing more colorful variants during meals and decided to look them up. As it turned out, bell peppers came in a whole range of colors—like orange, red, and yellow. The other colors tended to be less bitter than the green ones, and you could even eat them raw after washing.

Once Ayase took charge of the cooking, I started to see all sorts of new foods on our dinner table. Maybe the information Dad and I had was outdated. Broccoli and cauliflower were one thing, but we were definitely never going to encounter the fractal-looking Romanesco ordering takeout.

"You sure are good at improvising."

I was a little embarrassed about how I tended to just eat whatever she made without thinking about it.

"It's no big deal."

"I'm always grateful to you. I mean it. About finding you a high-paying job… Maybe I'll have to give up on that, but I'll spare no effort in supporting your bid for independence."

"You found that background music for studying, didn't you? I really appreciated that. So we're even," she said with a smile.

In that moment, the awkwardness of the past few days seemed to ease.

I saw Ayase dumping green tea leaves into a small teapot, so I reached into the cupboard and took out two teacups before placing them in front of her. She poured the tea, and we began eating.

The warm rice was tasty. As Ayase had said, it was nice and steamy, without any stickiness.

"There's more in the freezer. Help yourself if that isn't enough."

"It's pretty late. I'll make do with this."

I glanced at the clock on the wall—it was already past eleven. Time to finish dinner, take a bath, and go to bed. It might've been different during exams, but since Ayase took her baths after I did, she wouldn't be able to go to bed if I kept eating.

As we enjoyed a relaxing dinner, I found I wasn't sure what to do. The day was about to end, and I still hadn't gotten an answer from her. I sighed and made up my mind.

"Um… About Narasaka's pool party."

"That again?"

"You haven't passed me her contact information yet. If she's still waiting for my reply, I feel like it's about time I gave it to her."

"…Okay. Here." Looking a little grumpy, she picked up her phone from the table and started bringing up Narasaka's info.

"Wait." I held out the palm of my hand to stop her. "I don't care about Narasaka's contact information."

"…What?"

"In fact, I'm not that interested in going to the pool with her."

The suspicious look on Ayase's face turned to one of surprise. It was like she had no idea what had gotten into me—like she'd just gotten punched in the face from some crazy direction she hadn't anticipated.

That's right. I was about to say something crazy that she never would have expected.

I didn't mind that Ayase didn't want to go to the pool. And to respect her free will, I would simply have to wait until she changed her mind.

I considered interfering in someone else's decisions to be the conceited act of someone drunk on fiction and their own ego. Real life wasn't like fiction, and pretending otherwise was pathetic and an invitation to have it all blow up in your face. I knew that, and yet I was still worried about her.

"I want *you* to have fun at the pool."

"I don't understand what you're saying."

She was looking at me like I was a space alien—not that she'd know what one looked like, since I was pretty sure she'd never seen one. Ignoring that, I went on.

"Look, I said I wanted to go because I thought it might influence you to go, too. Then I asked you for Narasaka's contact info, thinking you might get jealous if you thought I was having fun without you."

"Who, me?"

"Yeah, you."

"Why would I get jealous?"

She looked like she was genuinely puzzled. I'd be extremely relieved if her face just then matched how she unconsciously felt inside.

"You want to go to the pool, don't you?"

Ayase closed her mouth. Then she pursed her lips as if she wasn't going to say another word no matter what.

"Akiko told me. She said that when you were a child, you hated the summer and would beg her to buy you ice cream or take you to the pool. You still don't like the heat, do you?"

"That's not..."

"It *is* true. That's why you went back to your room so quickly when our air conditioner broke down. You must be at least a little interested in going to the pool with your friend. Am I wrong?"

"Why do you want me to go to the pool so badly?"

"Didn't Dad say we'd have to study more once we become third-years, so we should enjoy ourselves while we still had the chance? You remember that, right?"

"Yeah, but..."

"I know you want to be independent as soon as possible. But at the rate you're going, you'll collapse before you get there. That worries me."

"You're worried about me...?"

"Yeah, I am. I want you to cut yourself some slack. And to do that, I think you need to take a break and let your hair down sometimes."

I'd said everything I wanted to say, so I simply waited for her response.

"I...don't know," she said, lowering her stylishly thin brows as she looked down at the table. "I don't have time for it. I really don't."

"Ayase..."

Ayase bit her lip and reached for the notepad on the table. Then she picked up a pen and wrote something while glancing at her phone. Finally, she slammed the notepad down on the table in front of me.

"I have to study."

With that, she took her bowls to the kitchen sink and then holed up in her room.

"Well, crap..."

Sighing, I glanced at the notepad in front of me.

Ayase had written down a phone number and scribbled **Maaya** under it. It must have been Narasaka's number.

"But there's no point in me going alone."

My shoulders sagged as I cleaned up my dishes and headed to my room.

●AUGUST 25 (TUESDAY)

After I woke up, I lay in bed thinking.

Had I made a mistake?

"Probably."

I said it to the ceiling, and with no one to hear me, my answer came echoing back down at me.

I turned over and checked the time. It was already noon, but I was still tired. I'd stayed up thinking the night before and wasn't able to get much sleep.

How was I supposed to overcome Ayase's stubbornness and get her to relax?

Stubborn… Yeah, that was it. She was determined—hardheaded even.

And that made her fragile.

Having lived with her for two months, I felt I'd gotten to know her somewhat. Now that I saw her almost every day at work, I was learning even more.

I figured she probably thought about things like this:

Children take the things they receive for granted, and because of that, they take more than they give. As a child, Ayase would ask her mom to buy her ice cream and take her to the pool. She was an average kid who simply took without giving. And that was perfectly natural.

But Ayase didn't agree with that, and that was the big issue.

Because of her family situation, she quit acting like a kid around the end of elementary school. She could no longer allow herself to be a child.

Society, for her, was based on give-and-take, and she'd decided to give more than she took.

Maybe she'd developed that policy because she felt guilty for always "taking" as a child—back when her mother had been struggling all alone. (Or at least, that was how Ayase saw it.)

Ayase wanted to grow up quickly and reduce the burden on her mom. For her, the time she'd spent "taking" as a child was shameful. She believed her childish selfishness had worsened the burden on Akiko.

How ironic.

Akiko had said herself that she wished Ayase had been able to spend more time as a carefree kid.

Thinking about it all made my heart feel heavy. Both Akiko and Ayase were thinking of each other, but they were working at cross-purposes.

The mother wanted her daughter to remain a child for a little longer.

The daughter wanted to grow up.

Their wishes contradicted each other.

Back then, they couldn't talk it out and come to a compromise, since Ayase had still been a child. Perhaps now that Ayase was older, they could manage it, but…

Ayase had started walking up the steps to adulthood while suppressing her own desires. She was shouldering her childhood like a debt she owed her mother, desperate to pay it back as fast as she could. All that had created the Ayase I knew, who blamed herself for everything.

That was why she couldn't relax—why she couldn't forget her responsibilities and just have fun.

She couldn't even forgive herself for wanting to go to the pool.

"I don't have time for it. I really don't."

She'd spoken with the same cool look she always wore, but I'd sensed a hint of desperation behind her words. That was why I couldn't say anything back.

If only I'd done something clever like a character in a novel or been more dramatic about it—maybe then she would have changed her mind.

No, that wasn't right. I couldn't simply run away from the problem. If I wanted to help, I had to get realistic.

The alarm at my bedside started ringing. It was about time I got up.

I turned it off with careless motions and pushed myself out of bed.

Once I was up, I realized it was halfway between breakfast and lunch.

I stood in the living room and wondered what to do. Should I eat something? Or should I try to hold out until lunch?

Normally, Ayase would have been up and made breakfast by the time Dad left for work, but she appeared to still be sleeping. I could tell by looking at the dining table. These things happened now and then, and our family didn't take it for granted that she would make breakfast for us every morning.

In fact, Dad and Akiko had told her not to push herself so hard during exams and had forbidden her from cooking for a little while.

Back to the matter at hand—how was I feeling?

I'm decently hungry. Maybe I can make some toast...

Just then, the door to the living room opened, and Ayase appeared.

"...Oh."

"Good morning, Ayase."

"...Morning."

She looked really tired, and her eyelids were drooping. Gone was the dignified atmosphere she always maintained, even at home. She was wearing looser clothes than usual; her armor seemed to be lacking in both attack and defense stats.

"Didn't you sleep?" I asked.

"I did...at around six AM."

I wouldn't call that sleeping. It sounded more like a nap.

"You should get some more sleep. You don't have work until evening."

"I'm fine... What time is it?" She sluggishly raised her head and looked at the clock. Her blurry eyes focused, then opened wide.

"What...?! It's already this late...?" She gasped and looked at the table. There was nothing there, of course. "I'm sorry. Dad didn't have anything to eat, did he?"

"It's okay. I think he had some bread."

A plate with a few breadcrumbs was sitting in the kitchen sink. He must have had toast, but it appeared he didn't have time to put his plate in the dishwasher, though he'd managed to put the butter and jam back in the fridge.

That was how we'd lived before Ayase and Akiko moved in. In fact, it was commendable that he'd eaten at all.

Ayase didn't need to feel guilty about it.

I said as much, but she didn't appear to hear me. She bit her lip like she'd messed up.

"I've never overslept like this before," she said.

"You're probably exhausted. Go back to bed and get some rest."

"I'll do no such thing… I'm really sorry! You haven't eaten yet, either, have you? I'll fix you something right away."

I could see bags under her eyes. She was way too tired for me to just say thanks and let her get to it.

"Ayase," I said, my tone serious and a bit formal.

"Y-yeah…?"

"I want you to hear me out, okay? Don't try to leave."

"Uh… What are you talking about?"

"Remember what you said when you first moved in?"

She gasped. She must have remembered. "…'It's nice that we can hash things out like this'…?"

I nodded. *Yeah, that.*

We were supposed to lay out all our cards from the start. We'd exchange information, share our emotions, and talk things out in order to get along. That was why I decided to tell her exactly how I felt.

"The way I see it, you are seriously lacking sleep. You can go ahead and argue, but take a look in the mirror. I don't want you forcing yourself to make breakfast when you're this tired. I'm worried that you'll get sick. You can sit in a chair if you like, and I'll fix breakfast. That's my honest opinion."

"Ngh… But I said I'd make breakfast."

"That might be the case normally, but we can be flexible. Your mission today is to sleep, not cook. That's my recommendation."

"B-but..."

"If you were acting the same as always, I wouldn't be saying this. But you said yourself that this is the first time you've slept so late, didn't you?"

"...Yeah."

"So this isn't a normal day. You don't need to push yourself to act the same as usual. Now sit down. Of course, you can always go to your room and go back to sleep."

As I spoke, I pulled back her usual chair, and it squeaked against the wooden floor.

"I'm just a little sleep-deprived."

"I know. And that gives you the right to sit in this chair. Come on."

"...Okay."

She gave up and sat down. I'd never seen Ayase look so weak.

"Think you can manage to eat a slice of toast?"

She nodded, and I tossed two slices—one for her and one for me—in the toaster. Next, I took butter and jam from the fridge and placed them in front of her, along with butter knives and spoons. I also got out some thinly sliced ham I'd found.

"Shall I grill the ham? I know you always do that."

"I like it better that way."

"You like it a bit charred, right?"

"...Yeah, I like it better that way."

"So do I. The charred part is nice and crunchy."

Since we were in agreement, I poured a little oil into a skillet and heated the ham on our induction stovetop. Once it started sizzling, I realized how hungry I was. Why did the sizzle of meat always wake up my appetite?

I placed the browned toast on a plate and carried it to the table. Then I put the charred ham on another plate and sprinkled it with black pepper, just as Ayase usually did. Wait a minute. Didn't she usually do that before she cooked it? ...Oh well.

I thought of something and opened the fridge. We had some leftover milk.

"Would you like some hot milk?"

"In this heat…?"

"It's cool in here with the air conditioner on. I thought it would be good to warm yourself up with a hot drink if you're going back to bed."

Ayase clammed up again, then said, "…Okay."

"Coming right up."

I poured milk into a cup, warmed it in the microwave, and placed it in front of her. Then I filled a glass with barley tea for myself and set it on the table. After that, I sat down and folded the palms of my hands together, indicating that I was about to dig in.

"Okay, let's eat. I probably should've gotten some vegetables out, too, but oh well."

"This is fine… Let's eat," she mumbled. She slathered her toast with butter, topped it with ham, and took a small bite.

I did the same, and we ate for a while in silence.

It didn't take long to finish a single thin slice of toast, though, and I saw that Ayase was now holding her mug with both hands and sipping her milk. I stared at my empty cup and debated whether to refill it.

Ayase exhaled, and it sounded like a sigh. Then she put down her mug. The small sound of it hitting the table echoed through the room.

"I've been thinking…" She took another small sip of her milk as if it were some special potion to give her courage. "…I don't mind going to the pool."

I'd been about to open the fridge to get more barley tea, but I quickly pulled back my hand and turned to look at Ayase.

"You've changed your mind?"

"I have now. Before I went to bed last night, I was sure I wouldn't go… No, that isn't right. I was debating it."

"Until six in the morning?"

"Until six in the morning."

"And now you've decided you want to go?"

She nodded. "I woke up today, and I felt…that maybe it was okay. But after everything I'd said, it was hard to admit."

When I heard her say that, all the strength drained from my body. I felt like a jellyfish in my chair.

I didn't need to do anything dramatic. Instead, Ayase had thought hard about it for one night—so hard that she couldn't sleep. When she finally got some rest and woke up again, her mind was changed. That was all it took.

Aha, so this is how it goes in real life. It felt strangely convincing. What you needed in the real world wasn't someone's Herculean effort. All it took was a simple sentence to trigger change. I'd read somewhere that people could rework their whole ideology over the tiniest things.

"But there's a problem," she said.

What?

"A serious problem," she continued, "that involves you as well."

"You can't swim? I'm not good enough to teach you."

"That won't be necessary. I can swim."

"Okay."

So that wasn't her problem. It must be even more dire—something big that had to do with me, too.

"I wasn't planning on going, so I agreed to work that day. I think you did, too."

"When's the pool party?"

"The twenty-seventh—the day after tomorrow."

"Whoa… Seriously?"

"Yeah. Seriously."

We were both off the next day, the twenty-sixth, and working the day after.

Well, crap. Ayase had finally changed her mind and decided to go, but at this rate, neither of us would be able to make it.

I thought about it for a few moments and decided to propose an extremely basic solution.

"Look, you've finally decided that you want to go. So let's make it happen."

"You think we can?"

"Well, stuff like this isn't that uncommon, so I think it'll be okay."

"You think so? I thought it'd be impossible…"

"Yeah. We'll just switch shifts with someone. Easy, right?"

It was a simple suggestion, and I tried to sound confident, but I was well aware that such things didn't always go smoothly.

It was half past four in Shibuya. The sunlight was coming in at a slant, and the scorching heat had eased ever so slightly.

I pushed my bike through the scent of burnt asphalt as I walked next to Ayase. I took the side closer to the road, with my bike between me and the passing cars.

We had decided to go to the bookstore early after agreeing that it would be bad form to ask the manager to change our shifts during work hours.

As I mentioned before, to commute together, either the person with the bicycle or the one walking had to match the other's pace. Neither Ayase nor I liked having to worry about such things. But that was only if there was no reason to do so.

I never imagined we'd be going to work together for a reason like this, though.

"Good. It's getting cloudy," Ayase said as she looked up.

She was right. Half the sky was now covered. It wasn't dark, since there were still patches of blue. But the air seemed slightly cooler and just a little less stifling.

Ayase, who had been fanning her face with one hand, stopped and repositioned her bag's strap where it lay on her shoulder. Her bag was quite full, since we had to take our work uniforms home with us.

Ayase's outfit that day made her look different.

She was wearing a bright, summery top with sleeves and a collar that didn't expose much skin. A narrow bow hung from where a guy would wear a tie. To borrow Ayase's armor analogy, I'd say it was an outfit with high defense stats and lower attack.

I'd told her we would need to be very polite when we negotiated. Maybe that was why she'd chosen this particular outfit. It made her look proper.

But the earrings that still shone at her ears seemed to say that she'd sting like a bee if you got careless. That was very like her. If I had to say more, she looked a little warm since she wasn't exposing as much skin.

"Are you okay? You aren't hot?"

"I'm fine now that it's clouded over."

"Did you get some sleep?"

"Yeah. Two hours."

Two hours didn't sound like enough, but there was no point getting into it again, and I didn't want to treat her like a little kid. My intention wasn't to turn her back into a child.

As I got lost in thought, the conversation petered out, and we walked in silence for a while.

When I began to hear the sounds of congested traffic and advertising trucks blasting loud music with no consideration for the local residents, I knew we were getting closer to Shibuya proper.

As the atmosphere around us began to change, Ayase spoke up.

"I'm sorry about yesterday."

"You mean about going to the pool?"

"That, too. But there's something else. I think I was a little nasty when you came to work with Yomiuri."

"Oh, that..." She meant the conversation I'd thought felt a little off.

"As his sister, I'm relieved he's found a wonderful person like you."

I'd laughed it off and assumed Ayase was joking, trying to amuse Yomiuri. But I knew she didn't like when people said that kind of thing, and so I'd wondered about it.

I would have assumed she'd be resistant to that kind of stereotype—that a boy and a girl walking together must be a couple. Even if she thought it, she'd probably insist it was wrong to say it to someone's face.

"I'd be breaking our promise if I felt weird about something and didn't tell you. It's okay; I'll be open about it. I can do it." She took her time converting her thoughts into words, like she was trying to convince herself. "How do I put this? I guess I just wanted you to tell me up front if you and Yomiuri were dating."

"Okay. But why?"

"I'm not sure... Let's leave it at that."

What a strange way to put it. Did that mean she knew the reason but couldn't tell me? It felt like Ayase was trying to pry into my relationship with Yomiuri, and she kept looking away from me. Both of those things seemed somehow meaningful, and I felt my heart begin to race in anticipation.

...Anticipation? Come on, Yuuta Asamura, what the heck are you anticipating?

I forced myself to calm down and quietly waited for Ayase to continue.

"Now that I've worked with her, I can tell that she's a really nice person."

"Yeah, she is."

"She's kind, attentive, smart, and knows everything, and she's fun to talk to—never boring."

"She's a bit of a slacker, and she's always telling dirty jokes, though."

"Those aren't flaws, Asamura. It's charming...but I don't have to tell you any of that. You've been working with her longer than I have," Ayase said with a wry smile. "Why the heck am I giving you a presentation on Yomiuri anyway?" I wanted to ask the same thing. What did Ayase really want to say to me?

"I guess I thought she'd make an acceptable sister-in-law. That's all. Sorry, I probably shouldn't have said something that might restrict you, but I just kind of blurted it out."

Without faltering, Ayase explained what had led to her reaction the day before. Her delivery was so smooth, in fact, that it felt like she was reading off some kind of mental cheat sheet she'd prepared in advance.

Was that *really* how she felt?

I forced myself to swallow back that question. Ayase had said she would tell me what had made her feel weird. If I doubted her, the whole basis of our relationship would fall apart.

In that case, I had no choice but to nod.

"Okay," I said. "I forgive you. So stop apologizing."

"Okay."

And so we put an end to our conversation and let it become water under the bridge… For Ayase and me, that was supposed to be the most comfortable way of doing things. But for some reason, I couldn't shake a weird sense of discomfort, like something was caught in my throat.

The crowds swelled as we approached the train station. Most office workers should still be at their jobs, and yet I could already see men in ties and hear the clacking of women's high heels mixed in with students still on summer break.

Then as I parked my bike, something occurred to me. I clicked my tongue. "Crap."

Ayase looked at me with surprise. "What's wrong?"

"Ayase, did you notice?"

"What?"

"I knew we would be going to work and coming home together. So why the heck did I bring my bike?" If we were going to be walking both ways, I could have just left it at home.

"Huh?" Ayase looked at me like she had no idea what I was talking about. "…Don't you have a reason?"

"Nope, none. I just brought it out of habit."

"W-well. These things happen, I guess… *Pfft!*"

"The power of habit is a little scary."

"Yeah. Let's leave it at that."

I could see the laughter in her eyes. Dammit, she was laughing at me.

Oh well… She'd been so tense lately; maybe it was better to have her smile, no matter what the reason.

I parked my bike and caught up with Ayase, and we went in through the employee entrance together. Inside, we spotted a senior worker and asked where the manager was.

When I opened the door to his office, he was there, sitting behind a desk by the window.

"Oh…? If it isn't the Asamuras… No, wait. You go by *Ayase*, don't you?"

I couldn't blame him for getting her name wrong, since she was Saki Asamura on paper.

Dad and Akiko were formally married, which meant everyone in our family now had the surname Asamura. But Ayase continued to use her old name at school and work out of convenience. That wasn't unusual, of course. I'd heard that more and more people continued to use their maiden names on business cards, e-mails, registers, and so on.

Since the bookstore was a new job full of new people, Ayase could have chosen to go by Saki Asamura, but apparently, she didn't want to get any special treatment as my sister. And because I called her Ayase, our coworkers had yet to find out that we were related.

"Hello, sir," I said. "Uh…"

"Hmm?"

When we didn't leave after saying hello, the manager looked up at us.

Despite his position, he was still only in his late thirties. He had a soft demeanor, but rumor had it that he was very skilled.

"Has something happened?" he asked.

"Um, sorry to spring this on you, but…Ayase and I are supposed to be off tomorrow and work the day after. Could we possibly have our shifts changed?"

"Oh…? This is sudden. Has something come up?"

"Well…"

It wasn't smart to lie at times like this, because if you were found out, you'd be done for. The important thing was to be honest but not to give out more information than you were asked.

So this is what I said:

"A friend of ours suddenly asked us to go on an excursion."

The manager knew we went to the same high school, so he would understand that it was our mutual friend. Ayase was the one close to Narasaka, and I barely counted as a friend, but I didn't need to explain any of that.

Ayase picked up from there.

"She was away on a trip until yesterday."

That was the truth. When I'd heard that, I realized why she hadn't contacted me. She'd already told Ayase about the pool party, so why would she bother calling or texting me while she was traveling?

There was a lie in our story, however. The invitation was only "sudden" for me, not for Ayase. That was why I'd been the one to handle that part of the explanation, while Ayase had brought up Narasaka's trip.

By doing things like that, it's possible to hide the truth without lying, though I don't particularly recommend it.

The important part came next: We had to convince him of our sincerity.

"I hate to trouble you, but would you please allow us to switch our workdays?" I bowed deeply, and Ayase followed suit.

"Hmm. Just a minute." At that, the manager started fiddling with his computer. He appeared to be looking at our work schedules. "Both of you, huh…?"

I raised my head and glanced at Ayase. She looked worried. What would happen now? If he turned us down, I'd have to start thinking about my next move. Of course, our request was legal, and he technically couldn't refuse, but I had no intention of getting pushy and souring my relationship with my boss… This didn't call for such drastic measures.

"The twenty-seventh, huh? That's Thursday. Hmm." The manager picked up the phone and made a call. After offering a brief explanation, he exchanged a few words with the person on the other end, then hung up. Then he repeated the process.

"Seems it's all right. We have two people with lots of experience and flexible schedules on tomorrow, and they said it would be no problem to cover for you."

"Really?!"

"Really." The manager smiled. "But I expect the two of you to work really hard to make up for it."

The manager was making good use of the carrot and the stick. An adult had the advantage when negotiating with a pair of high schoolers, of course. Maybe he'd even seen through our feeble excuse. But what mattered right now was letting Ayase have some fun. I'd do whatever I had to in order to make that happen.

Acknowledging our manager's warning, I said in my most serious voice, "We promise to give it our best!"

"Y-yes. We'll both work hard to make it up to you!"

Ayase and I bowed deeply once again, then left the manager's office.

Once the door had closed behind us, Ayase sighed.

"I'm so relieved," she said.

"I'm glad it worked out."

"I don't think I've ever felt so tense."

"Don't you think you're exaggerating a little?"

By the time we'd changed into our uniforms, our shift was about to start.

That day, we needed to shelve the additional books we'd ordered, so we stacked boxes filled with them on a trolley and wheeled it around the forestlike maze of bookshelves.

"Ayase, our next destination is…over there. These are new arrivals for the technical books section."

"Okay, Asamura."

Insisting that it was a waste of time to wait for me to follow with the trolley, she grabbed a few books from the box and hurried ahead to the shelf. She was already placing them into empty spots by the time I joined her and followed suit.

"The way you budget your time really helps out," I said.

"You're the impressive one. You know where every book belongs and how to get there efficiently."

"I don't have *everything* memorized."

Many of the books that had come in that day belonged to my favorite genres, which allowed me to come up with an efficient route through the store. I'd simply been lucky.

The boxes of books were empty at least fifteen minutes earlier than we'd planned.

"Okay, let's take a break," I suggested.

"All right."

We took the trolley to the back and headed for the break room. Ayase went to the ice tea dispenser, filled a paper cup, and took a seat.

"Asamura," Ayase said suddenly. She sounded less formal, maybe because we were the only ones in the break room. She downed her tea, stood up, and fetched herself another cupful. Then after settling down, she picked up where she left off. "The way I see it, it isn't that you can't make friends. You just don't."

"That's not my intention."

"But you don't really care that you don't have many, right?"

"Yeah, that's true."

"See?"

"Huh. In that sense, I guess you're right. I'm not exactly desperate to make friends."

That said, I didn't dislike having friends. I supposed I just accepted whoever came my way.

"To tell you the truth," Ayase began, "I didn't think the manager would change our shifts so easily. No…that's wrong. I was scared to negotiate. I didn't want to negotiate, so I made myself believe it wasn't possible."

"I'm just used to it. I've had shift changes a number of times before."

"Doesn't that mean you have more experience communicating than I do?"

I'd never even considered such a thing. "I guess…you could say that."

"You looked confident when we arrived at the store today and when you asked that other employee where the manager was. When you were negotiating with the manager, too, you stood firm and said what you wanted to say… You don't seem to me like someone who has trouble communicating."

"You give me too much credit."

I wasn't that good. I'd simply been working at the bookstore for a while, and since my coworkers and I shared a common topic—work—I was somehow able to make conversation.

"Work is a place where everyone's expected to be honest and sincere with one another," I said, "so it's a little easier is all. It's not as difficult to have the kind of clear dialogue you were talking about."

"I can't do it."

"Sure, you can. You just need to get used to working here. Actually, you're already there. I think it's much harder to communicate with friends, where there seem to be core rules established, but in reality, there aren't. I'm...not good at that. The way I see it, you're much better at it than I am."

"...Oh, come on."

It was true. I'd intentionally avoided saying it, but it was thanks to her ground rules that we were getting along so well as a family.

I couldn't tell her now that she'd finally decided to go to the pool, but at the moment, I was the one full of insecurities. I'd committed to accompanying her, but while I could talk to Ayase and maybe Narasaka, I had no confidence I'd be able to enjoy myself around our other classmates.

And the pool party was only two days away.

● AUGUST 26 (WEDNESDAY)

It was the morning of Wednesday, August 26, and summer break was almost over.

I'd set my alarm clock the previous night so I'd wake up around the same time Ayase usually did: six thirty AM.

...I was pretty tired.

I went to the living room to find Ayase already preparing breakfast.

I watched her for a while as she moved efficiently through the kitchen. I recalled what she'd said about having never slept in like the day before, and it rang true.

"Good morning, Ayase."

"Good morning, Asamura. You're up early today," she said, briefly turning around.

"Yeah. It's gonna be a busy day," I said, taking my seat.

Chop, chop... Chop.

Ayase stopped slicing carrots on the cutting board and turned around, looking worried.

"A busy day? All we did was switch our shifts. Do you have other plans?"

"Oh, nothing like that."

Ayase was probably concerned I'd had something else on my schedule and that changing our shifts for the pool party had caused me problems.

"You're sure?"

"I promise, I had the whole day off today. I was going to catch up with my schoolwork if I hadn't already done that, but that's out of the way."

"Then..."

Of course she was confused. How could she know? Mine was an issue unique to introverted high school guys like me.

"I don't have a swimsuit," I said.

"...How do you manage swimming at school?"

"...I always select ball sports instead of swimming, on the suggestion of a friend."

"Oh, I see."

"But I've learned my lesson. You lose out when you go along with everything your friend says."

I sagged my shoulders, thinking of Maru.

At our school, summer PE classes consisted of a choice between swimming or ball sports. Of course, I doubted that it would be cool to wear a school swimsuit to the pool with friends. Maybe it was just a false preconception, but I got the feeling there was a kind of dress code for when you went out with the popular kids.

"Ah-ha-ha, you're exaggerating. So you're going out to buy a swimsuit, huh?"

"Yep, I kind of have to. Fortunately, I can afford one, since I work. I get off at six PM today, so that should give me plenty of time to shop."

I was working mostly full shifts, so I usually got off pretty late at night. But that day, I would finish early, since it was the shift I would have been working on the twenty-seventh.

"You're going shopping after work?"

"I don't have a choice. I checked, but I couldn't find a store selling swimsuits that was open early in the morning. Most of them don't start up until eleven."

"Ah... And then you wouldn't get to work on time."

"I'd be cutting it close, at least, which I want to avoid."

I didn't want to be late for work right after the manager warned us that we had to do our best.

I could probably go to a store at eleven and get to work on time for my shift at noon—but only if I didn't have trouble choosing a swimsuit. And that was a big if.

"Do you think it'll be that hard? Oh, right… I forgot you aren't into fashion."

Precisely. I nodded, frowning.

Fashion was like my kryptonite. I had no idea how to choose. Why were there so many options? What was the difference? Was it like different genres of books? I could see myself standing stranded in a store. Who should I ask for help, and what should I say?

I was sure I'd wind up lost and confused. Rather than risk being late for work, I'd prefer to skip that anxiety and take my time.

I also had to get ready for the next day.

I didn't think going to a pool during break required that much preparation, but I didn't want to get there only to find out that I'd forgotten to bring this or that.

I'd told Ayase that I had the whole day off, but since I hadn't known I'd be working all afternoon and evening, I had a bunch of chores, like laundry, that I now had to do that morning.

"Okay, understood," she said. "Oh, hey, Maaya sent me the schedule for tomorrow."

"Oh yeah?"

"I'll forward it to you later."

"Okay."

We'd contacted Narasaka the day before to let her know we were going, of course. We'd waited until the last minute since we had to make sure we could change shifts. We couldn't tell her we were going and then send another message the same day saying we couldn't make it.

Ayase had texted her as soon we got permission from our manager, and she said the reply had come in less than a minute.

That was Narasaka for you.

While I thought about all this, I heard Dad wake up. It was almost seven AM. He made a stop at the washroom, then headed into the living room.

"Good morning, Saki. Oh, Yuuta. It's rare to see you up this early."

"Morning," I said.

"Morning," he said back as he took a seat.

I promptly got to my feet and filled his rice bowl. His disappointment was obvious.

Yeah, yeah, Dad. I bet you wanted Saki to do it. She'll bring your miso soup, so you'll have to make do with that.

"Here, Dad."

"Thanks, Saki."

"You're welcome."

Breakfast was Ayase's usual time-saving fare. That morning, it was boiled tofu and spinach covered with grated ginger, dried bonito shavings, and chopped green onions. Once we'd poured soy sauce over it, it was ready to eat.

I hadn't known this, but there were a lot of different vegetables similar to green onions that you could sprinkle on tofu. Ayase said the kind she was using that day were called "scallions." I did a little research online and found even more types: scallions, *wakenegi*, green onion shoots, chives, and green spring onions. I suddenly realized I had no idea what I'd been using all these years.

At any rate, the ones I was eating now were scallions.

In addition to the tofu, Ayase placed a blue plate in front of Dad with three *shishamo* fish on it.

"Yours will only take a minute, Asamura."

"Don't rush. Go ahead and eat, Dad."

If Ayase and I had school, we'd have to start eating soon or we'd be late. But right now, we were on break.

"Thanks, guys," Dad said and dug in.

He left at seven thirty sharp, and I tossed his bowl and plate in the dishwasher.

Shortly after he left, at around eight, Akiko came home. She went straight to her bedroom, saying she'd already eaten.

Ever since Akiko and Ayase had moved in, this was our typical breakfast routine. I thought back to how it had been when we were going to school. It was about time to start easing back into the old schedule, since summer break was almost over.

After helping with the dishes, I went to my room and checked the schedule for the following day until I had to go to work.

Ayase had forwarded me a number of messages from Narasaka. The next day's schedule was one long, single message. It was as detailed as a program for a school field trip.

Ayase said Narasaka had been traveling, and I wondered if she had started crafting it while she was away. Maybe she was the type who put everything into having fun.

An additional text from Ayase read:

Maaya went to the trouble of making this schedule, so read it carefully, okay?

Ayase had insisted she didn't want to go, but now she was extremely upbeat about it. It was just as Akiko had said.

"It was a nightmare when she was young. She'd beg for ice cream, make a fuss about going to the pool..."

It made me happy to think that Ayase was enjoying the prospect of having fun again.

Ayase and I left home a little before noon and arrived at the bookstore with plenty of time to spare.

"Okay, Ayase. Let's give it our all!"

"Yes. Let's do our best!"

As soon as we stepped inside, she started speaking more formally.

We worked even harder than usual as a way of thanking our manager for agreeing to switch our shifts.

We were asked to start ringing up sales the moment we began. The register was the most stressful of our tasks. You couldn't expect good communication skills from an introvert like me, but it was my job, and I had to do it.

When things got quiet at the register, we folded book covers using a piece of cardboard the same size as a book. First, we'd fold the top and bottom, then one of the sides. Since books come in all sizes, we couldn't fold both sides in advance, or the cover wouldn't fit. Technically, we could simply redo that fold, but we couldn't give customers a book with a creased cover.

Once, I'd made the mistake of folding both sides. Only certain books would fit in the covers I'd finished, and I had a hell of a time using them all up, not to mention I got chewed out for it. Ayase didn't make mistakes like that. She was a model worker—as Yomiuri said, she was even better than me.

That day, we also had to clean the back office and changing rooms.

Yomiuri was always gone when we had a bunch of tasks like this. I wondered if she had taken the day off on purpose, then realized I was supposed to be off as well.

"Okay," I said, "we'll be done once we take out this trash."

"I'll do it."

"Nah, I might as well finish up."

I was about to leave the office, plastic garbage bags in hand, when the manager walked in.

"Oh, everything is sparkling! Good job. I can tell you've worked hard." He showered both of us with praise.

I knew he was just saying it, but it felt good. He was skillfully offering us a carrot. The rumors were right—this guy knew what he was doing.

"Thank you," I said. I could see Ayase was smiling, too.

By six, we were both finished, and so we headed out together.

"Okay. Well, I'm off to get myself a swimsuit, so I can't walk you home today."

"You don't have to do that. It's only six o'clock."

"Good point. Well, hurry on home, then."

"Where do you plan on going?"

I told her the name of a department store where the chain I'd decided to visit had a shop.

"Oh, okay," she said. "I'll go with you."

My heart skipped a beat. "Why?"

"That department store has ladies' clothing shops, too. I'm also going to buy a swimsuit. I tried mine on yesterday, and I'm not sure it still fits right. So I thought, to be safe, I'd go ahead and get a new one."

With that, she took off walking. I quickly followed.

Were we really going shopping together? Based on my limited

experience and measly imagination, buying swimsuits together was a couple activity. I knew I was biased, but what other reason was there for a guy and a girl to go together? …I couldn't think of any.

Uneasily picking out swimwear, talking through the fitting room partition while trying things on, getting into weird predicaments—those were the kind of things you read about in novels and manga—they didn't happen in real life.

But Ayase's perfectly calm demeanor gave me the impression that perhaps I was just inexperienced, and it was an everyday occurrence for brothers and sisters to go out and buy swimsuits together.

But if we were really doing this, then how should I act? The store wasn't far. I wondered if I could finish preparing myself mentally by the time we got there…

As it turned out, I had no need to worry.

Department stores usually sold ladies' items on the lower floor and men's items upstairs.

Ayase stepped off the escalator on the proper floor, turned to me, and said, "Okay, this is where we split up. We'll meet up at the entrance if we happen to finish shopping at the same time. If not, we can head home separately without worrying about each other."

"…Okay."

That all made sense, of course. This was reality. It seemed I'd been right—an older brother had no reason to go swimsuit shopping with his sister.

Well…probably not anyway.

In the end, it took me more than an hour to choose a swimsuit.

What did I say? Coming after work was the right call.

● AUGUST 27 (THURSDAY)

I watched the scenery pass by under a blue sky as the train rocked beneath my feet.

It had been a while since I was last on one of these.

Born and raised in Shibuya, I had lived the life of a reclusive introvert and barely ever rode trains.

All I needed in life were manga and books. For a guy like me, Shibuya was a paradise. Even these days, when bookstores had all but vanished from smaller towns, Shibuya still had several large shops in operation.

I could kill time on my days off going from one bookstore to another, so there was no need to travel very far.

And yet here I was on a train, all so that I could go to the pool.

The train car wasn't very crowded. There were only five days of summer vacation left, including this one, and most people had stopped going out for excursions and started fretting about how little time they had left to enjoy their freedom.

I glanced at my cell phone and checked the clock: eighteen minutes after nine. I had plenty of time to get to Shinjuku Station by our nine-thirty meetup.

Once assembled, we would ride the train nonstop for half an hour, then take a bus for another thirty minutes. It seemed our destination was unexpectedly far away.

I was already starting to regret agreeing to go.

Come on, Yuuta, I told myself. *You can't abandon Ayase, turn tail, and run.*

Ayase had suggested that we arrive at the meeting point separately and had left more than fifteen minutes earlier than I had.

Since we acted like strangers at school, she didn't see any point in telling all our classmates the truth now.

Narasaka knew, however, and neither of us had asked her to keep it a secret. Even if she told people, it wouldn't exactly cause a problem.

So be it if people found out. It wasn't as if we were doing something wrong.

I absent-mindedly watched the scenery, lost in thought, until eventually, I heard the name of the station I was waiting for called out.

The doors opened with a *whoosh* as if the train were letting out a puff of air, and I stepped down onto the platform.

After passing through the ticket gate, I saw a group of about ten people. It was roughly half boys and half girls, and they all wore Suisei High School uniforms. They even had their bags with them, like this was some kind of school field trip.

"Weird," I mumbled.

I was in my uniform, too. Narasaka had texted me, saying to please be sure to bring my uniform and student ID. Maybe the idea was to get student discounts, but wouldn't our school ID's suffice?

Despite these lingering questions, I figured it would be better to wear my uniform than wear something else and stand out, so I decided to just go along with it.

Glancing around at the other students, I found I recognized a few of them.

"There she is..."

Ayase, also in her school uniform, stood a distance away from the crowd. She looked at me and breathed a small sigh of relief. She didn't have many friends, either, and from what I knew, Narasaka was the only one of our classmates she was close to.

Narasaka, on the other hand, was engaged in a lively chat at the center of the group. As expected of Suisei High's number one communicator (according to me). She noticed my arrival and stood on her tiptoes to wave in my direction. Looking at her small body stretched to the limit like that made me think of a prairie dog. She was cute in the way small animals were, and I guessed that was the reason she was popular with the guys.

"Asamura! Good morning, afternoon, and evening!"

"Good…morning, I think, should be enough."

"This is how you greet people in the industry."

"Which industry is that?"

"The Suisei High School industry."

"Oh, okay. I guess."

So high school was an industry. To be honest, I didn't really get it.

Everyone gave quick self-introductions, careful not to get in the way of the waves of people coming out through the ticket gates. The introductions themselves were short, but it took ages because Narasaka would make teasing remarks every time someone gave their name.

"I'm Yuuta Asamura… Hello."

"This is Asamura! He looks quiet, but his popularity is secretly on the rise!"

"How can you be secretly popular? Isn't that an oxymoron?!" one of the guys shot back, playing along with Narasaka's comedy routine.

"What I'm saying is that now's the time to make friends with him!"

The crowd laughed. Was it Narasaka's style to warm people up with jokes?

"Right, Asamura?!" she said.

"You got a lot of that wrong, but… Sure, whatever."

"Good to meet you, Asamura!" A big guy with a dark tan suddenly shook my hand. He looked like he belonged to the rugby team or something.

I froze for a moment—not because of his enormous size, but because we'd just met and he was already treating me like a friend. Was this the effect Narasaka had on people?

"Nice to meet you, too…," I said, squeezing his hand in return, though his friendliness made me a little uncomfortable. The guy seemed like a sports-loving extrovert with lots of friends, the exact opposite of me.

I managed to force myself to smile back at the cheerful stranger so that I wouldn't spoil the mood, but I felt totally out of my depth.

I wanted Ayase to have fun and feel refreshed, though, so I decided to do my best to blend in.

The self-introductions continued, and Narasaka chimed in for each one. With some people, she'd make puns or jokes; with others, she'd play the fool in ways that emphasized the name or characteristics of each person. Even I, a guy who wasn't much interested in remembering people's names, wound up learning several as well as a little bit about everyone's personalities. *So that's why she does it.* Maaya Narasaka was something else.

"I'm Saki Ayase."

"I think everyone knows Saki… Don't worry, she isn't as scary as she looks. She won't bite."

"Hi there."

"Call her Ayassie!"

What was that supposed to mean? It sounded like the name of a regional mascot.

"Please just call me Ayase," she said, unwilling to match Narasaka's energy. She didn't get mad, though, and I could make out a faint smile on her face, which seemed to surprise several other girls. They must have truly thought she was scary.

One of the students then asked a logical question: "Hey, Narasaka, why are we all in our school uniforms?"

"I told you. We wanna get those student discounts."

"Couldn't we just show our student ID cards?"

"That's just the official reason. Think about it! Even the strictest parents will allow their kids to leave the house if they're in uniform."

"I don't get it."

"Don't start sweating the small stuff; it's too much trouble. Besides, we've gotta enjoy these uniforms while we still can. Don't worry about it and just have fun."

The person asking the question didn't seem satisfied, but he backed down, unwilling to drag things out.

This brief exchange convinced me—Narasaka paid even greater attention to detail than I had thought.

At least one of the students here today probably had strict parents who wouldn't let them go out and have fun unless they lied and said they had to work on some school committee or something. They'd probably told

Narasaka beforehand, and she had arranged to have everyone come in their uniform so that person wouldn't stand out… All this was pure conjecture on my part, of course.

I glanced over the group. I had no idea who might've made the request. Narasaka was probably the only one who knew, and no one could tell because she did nothing to betray the secret. Dissatisfaction with this mystery rule would be directed only at Narasaka, and it didn't become a problem because she'd succeeded in creating an atmosphere that encouraged overlooking silly suggestions.

Once again, Maaya Narasaka's social skills proved to be on another level.

"Okay then, let's go!" she shouted.

With no one the wiser about her high-level machinations, Narasaka took the lead and began walking enthusiastically toward the train station ticket gates.

It was the start of a memorable summer experience—a field trip led by Ms. Narasaka, our teacher for the day.

We boarded our next train and headed west from Shinjuku.

About halfway to our destination, the skyscrapers began to disappear from view, and the windows filled up with blue sky.

Heading west from the city center meant we were moving in the opposite direction from Tokyo Bay, and it struck me as odd that we were headed away from the water in order to go swimming. But perhaps there were more pools farther inland precisely because it wasn't as close to the ocean.

Narasaka had assembled ten people, including Ayase and me—five guys and five girls. I was meeting seven of those people for the first time.

Surprisingly, I had no trouble conversing with them on the train. I'd been afraid I wouldn't be able to find topics to talk about, but that wasn't the case. Perhaps the mark of truly good social skills was the ability to match the pace of your conversation partner, even if that person was introverted or bad at talking.

"Oh, so you work part-time at a bookstore, Asamura?" someone asked.

"Yeah."

"Do you make good money?"

"I don't know… I've never worked anywhere else."

"Still, I'm impressed. You've been working all summer *and* taking summer classes. Wow!"

"Yeah," someone else chimed in. "All *I* did was sleep the summer away!"

"Oh, it's nothing to be impressed about…," I replied.

I still wasn't good at so-called idle chitchat.

I could talk forever about my favorite books. But I supposed it wasn't exactly a conversation if I just went on and on. That said, I found it pretty difficult to pass information back and forth without first establishing a theme.

At any rate, I somehow got through all the small talk, and after half an hour on the train and another thirty minutes on a bus, we arrived at the front gate of the pool complex.

It was blazing outside, and when we stepped off the bus, a blast of hot air enveloped us, making me dizzy. The difference in the temperature between the air-conditioned bus and the outside was too much. The white lines on the asphalt below our feet reflected the sun's rays, blinding me.

"This is it?" I said as I looked up at the enormous building before us.

The only pools I knew were the one at our school and the local community pool. The gigantic structure in front of us seemed more like a hot spring resort or something.

"This is the entrance," said Narasaka. "They have a big indoor pool under a transparent roof and an outdoor pool on the other side. Look over there. You can see part of it from here."

"Oh…a slide."

"At least call it a waterslide! Come on, Asamura, get in the spirit!"

"I don't think spirit has anything to do with it."

"What would people think if high schoolers like us went home and said we'd played around on a slide all day?!"

"Wouldn't they just think we'd played on a slide?"

Narasaka turned to Ayase and the girl next to her. "…Saki. Yumi. Say something!"

"It's a little big to just call it a slide," said Ayase. "So I think it would be more accurate to call it a really big slide with some water flowing over it."

Ayase was just providing a description at this point.

Yumi Tabata widened her eyes. (I remembered her name because it was the same as a train station on the Yamanote Line, as Narasaka had mentioned in her introduction.) "I had no idea you told jokes, Ayase."

"Jokes… Um, yeah."

Ayase didn't tell jokes. She was only saying what was on her mind.

"They even have an amusement park behind the outdoor pool," Narasaka continued. "Hey, Asamura, is this your first time at a place like this?"

"Uh, I guess it is."

It wasn't that I disliked amusement parks or zoos. I was actually quite fond of them. What I didn't like was having to match another person's pace at attractions, fairs, festivals, and so on. I would much rather visit them alone.

Perhaps that was what made me an introvert, but everybody has their own pace. Why did everyone seem so eager to rush around like they were being chased?

"Today, we're going to focus on the indoor pool!"

"Oh, right."

It said as much in the schedule Narasaka had sent out.

We paid for day passes at the entrance and went inside. I got changed in the men's changing room and put on the brand-new swimsuit I had bought the day before.

I wasn't particularly embarrassed—it was no different from changing into my gym clothes at school. But the locker key was a concern. It was attached to an elastic band, which you were supposed to wear around your wrist and take into the pool. What if it came off and drifted away in the water? Was no one else worried? Or was I overthinking things?

Anyway, once I'd changed into my swimsuit, I headed for the pool building.

When I stepped inside, I was stunned.

It was like a huge greenhouse. And that wasn't clear plastic surrounding the pool. It had to be glass or maybe plexiglass.

The pool was gigantic. Several of our school's gyms would fit inside, though I couldn't be sure how many. A massive, shallow pool made up about a third of the area, equipped with a wave machine that sent water rolling from one end to the other. There was a slide, of course—or rather, a *waterslide*, as well as various contraptions whose use eluded me.

The whole place had that unique pool smell, different from the ocean.

A fair number of people were there, though not as many as I had imagined. Perhaps I should have expected as much for a weekday at the end of summer vacation. I was glad it wasn't crowded.

I met up with the girls. You could tell that all five of them were wearing brand-new swimsuits. I remembered what Ayase had said the day before. *I guess girls really pay attention to this stuff.* And here I was, only considering buying new clothes when I ran out of stuff to wear.

Narasaka wore a bikini that showed lots of skin. Its lemon-yellow color suited her bright personality. But perhaps because of her mannerisms and the fact that she was a little short, it wasn't as sexy as you might imagine. It was more on the cute side.

In contrast, Ayase's swimsuit was a tank top bikini. Her shoulders were bare, but there was no space between the top and bottom, which were fastened with strings.

Probably because it was hot, Ayase liked to have her shoulders bare. I'd seen them almost every day, yet my heart skipped a beat when I caught sight of her in a swimsuit. While it was hardly a change from what I was used to, I was powerfully aware that this was a completely different type of outfit.

"Wow!" The guys hollered in unison when they got a glimpse of the girls. I didn't have much interest in such things, but even I could tell that the most intense gazes were focused on Ayase.

Her figure was completely different from the others. She had a high waistline, and her legs were long and slender. All that was obvious, despite her modest swimsuit. I heard quiet whistles from the guys and felt a strange emotion rise inside me that was hard to describe. What the heck was I feeling?

"Look at Ayase. Wow! Hey, Asamura, don't you agree?"

"I'm not sure it's...good to talk about her in a lewd way," I said on reflex.

These days, it was better to watch what you said. If you were careless, you might find yourself accused of harassment. That was part of my reasoning, but there was something else. The vague, unpleasant feeling welling up within me was also a big contributor.

It didn't seem like anyone else agreed, however.

"Oh, come on. Any guy would look at that! Right?"

"There's no point in resisting!"

They went on and on. I wasn't sure if they could tell how annoyed I was or not. But just as I was about to tell them off, Narasaka interjected.

With her left hand on her hip, she pointed at us with the other. "Okay, you guys over there! Asamura is right! I'll crush your eyes and blind you if you keep looking at us with those lewd stares!"

Narasaka stuck out her middle and index fingers, indicating that she was ready to attack. *She looks pretty intimidating.*

At any rate, she'd managed to shut the guys up. It seemed they'd also noticed the frosty looks on the girls' faces as they stared at them.

I was a typical teenage boy, too. I might be an introvert, but I understood how they felt. That said, you had to remember not to say stuff like that in front of girls in this day and age. Not that I was confident in the high-mindedness of my own clumsy, spur-of-the-moment statement.

I sensed someone's eyes on me and turned just in time to see Ayase look away. Had she been...watching me? I couldn't know for sure. She immediately went toward the girls and mixed in with them.

"Okay, people, let's pull ourselves together and have fun!" Narasaka declared energetically, bringing heat back to the frigid atmosphere. "We're going to go around and see everything until lunchtime! Let's start with that giant slide!"

She pointed to the waterslide.

...So now it's okay to call it a slide?

According to the document Narasaka had sent out, titled Let's Make Summer Memories! Schedule, we were supposed to spend the morning going around all the attractions.

We began with the waterslide. It was small compared with the one outdoors that we'd seen from the entrance, but it was still two stories tall and plenty thrilling. Next, we waded beneath a waterfall and got lost in a maze, cheering now and then as we made it through each attraction.

I recalled the schedule that Narasaka had outlined and was amazed by her attention to detail. These types of attractions guaranteed a good time. To put it a different way, they provided a solid level of fun for everyone who participated.

The ten people who came along that day hadn't known each other very well. Making sure everyone was meeting for the first time ensured that preestablished friend groups didn't clump together, leaving others out. Ayase and I were a little different, of course—we already knew each other.

Even though we all went to the same high school, there was no way that ten students from different classes would suddenly become friends, and Narasaka knew a pretty diverse group of people to begin with: sporty people, those interested in the arts and culture, people she knew from committees, and those with similar hobbies. Any communication beyond small talk was going to be difficult, since we had nothing in common.

But Narasaka must have considered that. And her answer was to first have everyone tour the attractions, which were guaranteed to be fun, as a group. Everyone was sure to enjoy themselves, and the experience itself would become a shared topic of conversation. That would ensure a good atmosphere at lunch.

That was why she'd had us walk around first and waited until the afternoon to schedule her own events. It seemed Narasaka had a few ideas of her own for later that would see the boys and girls playing together.

This type of planning might seem easy, but it really wasn't. If you organize an event yourself, you tend to believe it will be more interesting than anything else. But Narasaka had intentionally scheduled those things for later. If everyone got too excited or something went wrong and we ran out of time, they could be cut entirely. (It even said so on the schedule.) That wasn't something you could do unless you were thinking about the participants first instead of what you wanted.

We decided to have lunch a little after twelve, when we noticed a good space open up in the eating area. I could tell the others were enjoying themselves talking about what we'd done that morning. Narasaka's plan had gone perfectly.

As for myself, I was glad to see Ayase laughing with the other girls.

We finished eating, rested for a while, then decided to go to the big, shallow pool.

Perhaps because it was a weekday at the end of summer vacation, there weren't many people in it, and we were able to have fun together as a group among the waves.

Unlike the beach, we couldn't play volleyball or build things with sand. That limited our activities, but Narasaka had helpfully listed a number of things we could do in her schedule.

"Now, people, we're going to play kickboard Othello!"

"Okay!"

Everyone responded enthusiastically, like we were back in elementary school. Even Ayase opened her mouth wide to shout her agreement, though it was a little flatter and quieter than the others. I chuckled inwardly. It kind of sounded like she was groaning.

I don't know if Kickboard Othello was the official name of the game or a Maaya Narasaka original, but the rules were simple. We each got a kickboard with different colors on either side. Fortunately, the pool had these available. Then we floated them on the water's surface, half with the top part showing and the other half reversed, and divided ourselves into two groups.

"We'll form two teams with a quick game of rock-paper-scissors," said Narasaka. "Winners come over here, and losers go on that side."

We were all set, with five against five. The winners became the "top" team, and the losers were the "bottom" team. By sheer coincidence, Ayase and I ended up on the same team. Narasaka would be one of our opponents.

"I'm going to set the timer now. We have three minutes," she explained. "The top team wins if more boards are topside up, and the bottom team wins if it's the reverse."

"Okay."

"Got it!"

"You aren't allowed to grab or clutch the boards. They have to be floating, and you can only hit the ends to flip them over. But you *can* push the boards away to keep your opponents from hitting them. Like this." She pushed a board to make it float off. "Is everything clear?"

"Yeah!"

"Guys! No cheating!" Tabata warned.

"Of course not. Don't you trust us?" a boy said sulkily. Was his name Myoujin?

Narasaka set the timer on her smartphone, which she'd placed in a waterproof case. She then declared the game underway, and we began playing at the edge of the pool.

It was tougher than I'd expected. Were you really supposed to play this in a pool with a wave machine? The boards kept floating away, even if we didn't do anything. And since we weren't allowed to grab them, someone had to keep pushing them so that they stayed in our area.

Eventually, we divided up into those who waited for the boards to float away and pushed them back toward the group, and those who hit them to turn them over. You could say we adapted to the environment.

After a while, we heard a cheerful melody erupt from Narasaka's phone. Our three minutes were up.

"Okay, stop! No more hitting the boards!"

Everyone froze.

Ayase's and my team won with a score of six to four. The winners cheered, and the losers splashed in frustration. Everyone had competed earnestly, and we were all out of breath.

"Okay, guys. Let's go another round!" Narasaka said after resetting her timer.

Everyone talked heatedly about winning the next game.

Incidentally...though no one else seemed to notice, Narasaka's timer was set to music I recognized. It was the opening theme for an anime. I knew it because I had watched it last season on Maru's recommendation. So Narasaka was into anime, too. She sure had a wide range of interests.

We lost the second round.

Neither Ayase nor I was into physical exercise, and our bodies couldn't hold out. With two of our five players useless, we were no match for the more active players and sports team members on the other side.

"Okay, that's the end of the event!" Narasaka called out. "Let's take a break, and then you're free to do whatever you want! Be back here at four, and we'll start packing up!"

After that, I slumped by the pool.

Man. I must have used a bunch of muscles that didn't usually see much action, and I was so exhausted, I didn't want to take another step. I wanted to lie down on the spot.

I couldn't work up the energy to follow the lively bunch who ran off saying they'd go around the attractions again. As I lay there without doing anything, Ayase approached me.

I forced myself to get up as she peered into my face. She looked a little worried.

"Are you okay?" she asked.

"Yeah. Just tired. I'm amazed by everyone here. They've got great endurance and excellent reflexes."

There were a handful of girls who had been the stars of the show all day—I suspected this group went out and did things a lot. I was basically a homebody, so I hadn't had much of a chance to show off. Not that I really cared about stuff like that.

"Well, you were pretty cool just now."

"Huh?" Ayase's words had caught me totally off guard.

"That game with the kickboards. You kept pushing them back into our play area and never let up."

"Oh, that."

Well, I had to do that, or we wouldn't be able to play the game. And once the others noticed, more people came to help.

Ayase slowly shook her head. "But you were the first to think of it. You left hitting the boards and flipping them to the others when that was the most enjoyable part of the game."

I was stunned. I didn't think anyone had noticed.

When boards came floating my way, if they were topside up, all I had to do was shove them back toward my teammates. The problem was when the bottom side was facing up. It was more efficient to hit them and turn them over before pushing them back. That was what the game was all about, after all. But when a teammate was nearby, I'd say, "*It's all yours,*" and let them do the flipping.

Why did I do that? Because that was the fun part, just as Ayase said.

I could have kept hitting the boards that the waves floated toward me, but that wouldn't have been fun for everyone else. It was a team event, after all.

"Well, to be honest, I just didn't want to take the risk of standing out and then mess it up."

Part of that was true.

"Really? Well, I don't care what the facts are. I only wanted to commend you. I thought it was cool. That's all. You were like a stagehand who spends all his time making the actors look good."

"Is someone like that cool?"

"I guess that varies from person to person."

"Huh… I guess that's true, but having someone say it to my face is kind of embarrassing."

I saw the corners of Ayase's lips turn up a little.

It wasn't the polite smile she directed at Dad or the aloof expressions I saw at home. If I had to say, it was an innocent smile that resembled the one in her childhood photo.

Ah, I'm so glad I pushed myself to come.

My feelings weren't arrogant satisfaction at having saved Ayase from a breakdown.

No, I was happy because if I had kept my distance like I'd said, I never would have seen her smile like that. I felt a silly sense of superiority, knowing I was the only one to see that smile in this moment. I'd done this for me and me alone.

"So that's all I havc to say," Ayase said, standing up. I turned to look at her as she rose. "Well, off I go."

Her swimsuit was still damp, and it was a darker color than when it was dry. A few drops of water remained on what little of her skin was showing, reflecting the light. She shook her head, flinging them around.

"I think I'll go for another swim!" She clasped her hands together, raised them above her head, and stretched.

"...Huh?"

In that moment, I suddenly realized something.

I wonder what it was. It felt completely natural. Out of nowhere, an emotion bubbled up inside me.

Oh. I love her.

The words came to me first. Then came the shock at what I was feeling.

I'd had plenty of opportunities to come to this realization. Why had it taken something so trivial—a gesture of hers I must have seen any number of times before—to make me understand?

All she'd done was clasp her hands together and stretch her arms. That was it.

It wasn't as if she had professed her love to me or we'd overcome some hardship together.

I'd heard classmates talk about this stuff at school—so-and-so fell for so-and-so, or so-and-so confessed their feelings. I'd listened to it vacantly, thinking it had nothing to do with me. How could I have ever imagined I'd wind up experiencing it myself?

In all honesty, I found women difficult.

Having grown up with my mom and dad, I had no illusions about getting married and living happily ever after. I had a sober view of relationships between men and women. I'd watched my mom yell at my dad for not shutting up or not reading her mind. I'd listened to her nag him about always being a perfect gentleman. Then when he'd try to be considerate, she'd get mad about him being too passive and not manly enough. And after all that, she'd cheated on him and run off with some rich guy she apparently thought was more macho.

That was how I envisioned all relationships and why I'd never fallen in love with anyone.

Why now? And why her, of all people?

The changes I felt inside were too real and too sudden, and I couldn't keep up. I didn't understand.

Most people say feelings of love are wonderful and precious. I had no idea they'd hit me so suddenly, in a single instant, like bubbles bursting to the surface of my mind.

As I watched Ayase walking away—water dripping down her back, making it shimmer—a thought occurred to me.

She's my younger sister.

But at the same time, she's Ayase.

She's my stepsibling.

We started packing up at four PM.

I put on my regular clothes in the changing room and realized at once how exhausted I was. My body was warm. I felt feverish and heavy like I'd just stepped out of a hot bath. It was the same kind of exhaustion I'd always felt after swimming class at school.

The guys assembled at the exit, ahead of the girls. I figured that since a lot of girls had longer hair, it probably took more time to dry.

We got on a bus that left at five sharp and said our farewells to the pool.

We went back the same way we'd come—thirty minutes on the bus and then another thirty on the train. Because of the time we'd spent together at the pool, we were much more talkative on our way back.

It was past six by the time we arrived at Shinjuku, where we would go our separate ways. When I walked past the ticket gate, I saw the sky on the other side of the road outside. It was still the crimson of sunset, but the sun had moved pretty far to the west.

As I gazed at the tall buildings blocking out the sky, I felt like I was home—back in this city full of skyscrapers.

"Boy, we had a lot of fun!"

"Maaya, you look like you could go a few more rounds."

"Uh-uh. I'm hungry!"

Everyone laughed at Narasaka's honest response.

We were about to split up. Some of us would board buses, others would take one of several rail lines, and still others would ride home on their bicycles.

Ayase and I would be taking the train to Shibuya Station, and from there, I would ride my bike, and Ayase would walk. We'd be leaving the group together, saying we lived in the same direction. No one would guess that we were headed to the same apartment.

"Okay, see you guys at school!"

Saying cheerful good-byes, we all set off in different directions.

"Oh, Asamura. Hold on a sec!" Narasaka gestured for me to come over, so I did.

"What is it?"

"I think this is a good opportunity to exchange contact info. How about it?"

I reflexively glanced at Ayase. She quickly looked away, but she hadn't been glaring at me or anything—probably not anyway. Narasaka and I went to the same school, so I figured it wasn't too weird.

"Okay," I said. "We might as well."

Once we'd exchanged info, I looked up at her.

"Thanks for putting together today's schedule, Narasaka."

"Hmm? You make it sound like we barely know each other. Call me Maaya!"

"We aren't that close yet."

"We aren't?! We just went to the pool together. We're like best friends now!"

I had a hard time following her logic.

"Oh, I wanted to say that I could tell you put a lot of effort into that schedule. You had us go around the attractions first, which made for lively conversation at lunch. It's just a shame that we could only play one of the games you planned."

"Huh." She scratched the back of her head, looking slightly embarrassed. "Well. It couldn't be helped since we were running short on time."

"But thanks to you, even I had a great day. I really appreciate it."

"Hey, flattery won't get you anywhere."

"I'm not trying to get anywhere. I'm saying this because I mean it."

"Huh, well, it's nice to hear. Wah-ha-ha-ha. I didn't expect it or anything, but it makes me happy that someone was paying attention."

"I think I get that."

...It was nice to have someone pay attention and notice the things you did. I had someone like that, too.

"Okay then, later!" Narasaka said. "See you, Saki! I'll text you!"

"Okay."

Narasaka and Ayase waved to each other. The former turned around several times and waved some more, before finally walking away, a bounce in her step.

"Sorry to keep you waiting," I said to Ayase.

"Mm. You didn't take that long."

Ayase and I passed through a ticket gate together on our way to our next train. For some reason, we were both silent on the ride back. We exited at Shibuya Station and began walking toward our apartment building. I got my bike from the parking lot where I'd left it, then walked side by side with Ayase, pushing it along.

The sky was changing color from crimson to dark blue, and the scenery around us was dim and shadowy, though our path was lit by the surrounding buildings.

It was that particular kind of light you got at dusk and dawn. In Japanese, the words for both meant "the time when you can't make out people's faces." Unless you ask, you can't be sure who's near you. I liked these words; they made me feel like strange beings might be walking among us—humanlike, but really something else.

In fact, there was another word in Japanese for this time when the sun sets and the sky turns dark, and it isn't quite day or night. According to folk tradition, *omagatoki* was "the hour for meeting ghouls and monsters." It was times like that when you began to worry if the person standing next to you was really who you thought they were—a time when reality seemed unreal...

"You've gotten pretty close to Maaya," Ayase said, pulling me out of my musings.

"Oh, uh, yeah. I wanted to thank her for inviting me."

"Thanks."

"Hmm?"

"She's my friend. So I'm happy you praised her."

We hadn't been that far away, and it seemed like Ayase had overheard us. I hadn't said anything I didn't want her to hear, but I felt a strange sense of guilt.

"Anyway, did you enjoy yourself?" I asked.

"Yeah, thanks to you," she said, bowing slightly.

"I used to enjoy going to swimming pools," she added, mentioning it had been a while since she'd last done it. "It was fun, and it felt good to go swimming again. I'm glad I listened to you," she said with a smile.

Watching her, I recalled the indescribable emotion I'd felt earlier.

I was troubled by my newfound feelings for the girl walking next to me—feelings of love, or at least attraction.

Seeing her that way would destroy the trust we had nurtured. And if I told her, she'd have no idea what to do. But at the same time, I got the feeling Ayase harbored a kind of fondness toward me, too. What was the right thing to do here?

I was talking less and less as I began to lose myself in a maze of emotions. Apparently, the silence was infectious, and Ayase grew quiet, too.

The sound of her footsteps matched mine, and all we could hear was the squeaking of my bicycle tires as they rotated.

I couldn't bear to look at her face. I kept staring at the ground. I could no longer tell what she was gazing at as she walked.

I felt my heart begin to race. Was that natural when you were walking alone with a pretty girl at dusk?

No. I'd gone to a late-night movie with Yomiuri the other day. I was nervous then, too, but I could say with confidence that it wasn't like this. Because it happened recently, the difference was as clear as day.

But if you asked me what was different…I couldn't say. I felt pathetic. I wanted to bury my face in my hands. Somehow, I instinctively knew it wasn't the same. The mechanism, however, was locked away in an impenetrable black box. These were my emotions, and yet I had no idea what was going on.

As I watched my bike tire roll across the asphalt at a steady pace, I noticed its shadow grow darker and darker. I looked up at the sky and saw that night had fallen without me realizing it. As I thought about how short the dusk had been, words bubbled up in my mind.

Ah, the moon is so beautiful.

"You're good at noticing people's strengths, Asamura."

"Huh?"

Her words seemed to come out of the blue, and I glanced over at her. Ayase was looking up at the sky, too. She was probably also gazing at the moon.

Then she turned to face me.

"I mean about Maaya. You praised her earlier."

"Oh, that."

"You really pay attention to people. I respect that."

"You…think so?"

"Yeah, I do. You pay attention to others' efforts. Like I said at that pool, I think that's cool. I really admire that…"

She was piling on the praise, making my heart beat even faster. But what she said next rendered me speechless.

"…Big Brother."

I swallowed. I was frozen in place, still staring at her face. Her familiar profile looked like that of a total stranger.

Big Brother.

Big Brother.

Big Brother.

I chewed the words over in my mind, but no matter how many times I repeated them, the meaning didn't change.

Big Brother.

In other words, she saw me as her brother.

I had never heard her say those words before. I had no idea why she was saying them now.

But why was I so surprised? She was the only girl in the world who could logically call me that.

"Um, did I surprise you by saying that all of a sudden? But you've been thinking of me and doing a lot for me—like a real older brother I can depend on…" Ayase tilted her head to the side and smiled.

There's no way I could tell her how that really made me feel.

"Well… It makes me happy to hear you say that, Ayase."

"…Ah-ha-ha. But it still doesn't quite feel right."

To be honest, she'd saved me.

The unexpected "Big Brother" had brought me back to my senses. What on earth had I been thinking? Sure, Ayase treated me warmly, and yeah, she praised me—but that was because I was her *older brother*.

She trusted me as someone she could have a neutral relationship with. She found me easy to get along with because I didn't get my hopes up or have lewd thoughts about her. She considered our relationship convenient for those reasons.

And here I was, about to break all the rules.

"I'm tired today," she said. "Do you mind if I make something simple for dinner?"

"…Sure. No problem."

Even innocent daily exchanges now terrified me. Was I speaking with my usual calmness?

When we arrived at our apartment building, I said I was going to park my bike, and we split up at the entrance. I took my bike to the roofed cycle shelter, locked it, and looked up at the sky.

The tall walls of the building blocked my view, and I could no longer see the moon.

I took a deep breath and told myself to settle down.

Ayase wasn't anywhere nearby. If I was simply attracted to her appearance or her pheromones or whatever, then without her in front of me, the

flames of passion that had risen inside me should gradually fade away. Then I could tell myself that those feelings, whatever they were, had only been a kind of momentary confusion and forget about them.

"Crap..."

I knew this was no good. I knew I wasn't supposed to have these feelings, and yet they just wouldn't go away.

"How am I supposed to go home and face her...?"

There was no one to tell me the answer. Of course there wasn't.

This was something I couldn't let anyone else overhear.

●AUGUST 28 (FRIDAY)

"Now I've done it..."

When had I last slept in like this?

I hadn't just woken up after noon; I'd missed the start time for my summer classes. I silently apologized to Dad for being a terrible son and playing hooky after he paid for my course.

I hadn't slept a wink the previous night. Ayase and I ate dinner together, but our conversation was awkward, and the atmosphere felt strange. When I got into bed, I kept thinking back to the things we'd done that day and my memories of Ayase, and that had kept me wide awake.

Argh. What the heck am I doing?

I was thirsty. I wanted something to drink.

Scratching my head and making my bed hair even worse, I went into the living room, too lazy to wash my face, and heard a woman's pleasant voice.

"Good morning, Yuuta."

"Huh? Akiko? And...Dad?"

"Hey. Morning."

Dad looked up from his tablet, where he was reading something (probably an online newspaper), and waved.

Two glasses of iced coffee sat on the table in front of them. The television was on, tuned to a high-budget foreign drama. It was a pleasant, comfortable morning scene.

"Yuuta?" asked Akiko.

"Oh...excuse me. Good morning."

I'd been standing there in a daze, but I quickly greeted them once I noticed their concerned looks.

I fled to the kitchen, opened the refrigerator, and pulled out the barley tea. I poured myself a glass and drank it in one gulp, like a traveler in the desert who had just found an oasis.

Drinking the cold tea in the air-conditioned room seemed to cool my brain, and my mind cleared up.

"Why are you both at home today?"

"Akiko and I discussed things," Dad said. "We both took PTO on Friday, Monday, and Tuesday so we'd be off at the same time, as a little summer vacation."

"Oh, I see. You're running a bit late for summer vacation."

"I wasn't going to take any since my superior doesn't like it when I stay away from the office too long, but Akiko insisted."

"Sorry to push, Taichi. I just thought the four of us could relax as a family if we had some time off."

"The four of us, as a family...," I mumbled.

"Saki told me you took yesterday and today off work," said Akiko.

She was right.

It was a good thing Ayase and I both happened to have the day off. It would be suicidal to go to work exhausted from the pool on a day as busy as Friday.

Myself aside, I figured Ayase wouldn't be able to fully enjoy herself if she thought she had to conserve her energy.

"Judging by the time," Dad noted, "it looks like you're skipping class today, too. Ha-ha-ha."

"You knew that and didn't wake me?"

"Always studying, working—I think you're a little too serious. It's good to have days like this now and then."

"I guess it could be worse..."

"Tee-hee. I hope you'll indulge us and leave it at that," said Akiko.

Dad wasn't the only one acting irresponsible. Akiko said she'd make me some breakfast and went to the kitchen.

My new mother splashed some oil into a skillet and looked at me with big, bright eyes. "Thanks, Yuuta."

"Huh?"

"For taking Saki to the pool."

"Oh… That wasn't me. Ayase's friend was the one who invited her."

"But she probably wouldn't have gone if you hadn't pushed her."

"…Maybe not."

"So thanks. It's so reassuring having you as her older brother."

My heart skipped a beat.

She probably didn't mean anything by it, but the words *older brother* came across like a condemnation of my improper feelings.

"You have less than two years before you both graduate from high school—two more years until she leaves home. It's a little sad to think that we don't have much time left to spend relaxing together as a family."

Akiko smiled sadly, and I gasped.

Time spent relaxing together as a family.

It was a small wish, but it probably meant the world to Akiko. Ditto for Dad.

Here was a man and a woman who had both been through failed marriages and had little experience being part of a happy family. No wonder they treasured these casual family gatherings.

What would they think if they found out that I was attracted to Ayase?

They had been through a lot, suffered, and finally found happiness. Did I have the right to spoil all that with my crazy, selfish emotional outburst?

Of course not.

An image of my biological mother flashed across my mind. This was the woman who'd had Dad wrapped around her little finger. He had been devoted to her and worked like a dog, at the mercy of her every whim. This was the woman who, in the end, met another man and ran off with him. I despised her. I used to think she was like an animal, unable to control herself.

It wasn't like I was wholly dedicated to my dad, but I didn't want to become someone who let his life be dictated by his own selfish feelings.

Could put a lid on the emotions budding inside me? I'd be lying if I said yes.

But I had no choice in the matter. I had to keep these feelings to myself and slowly try to wipe them away.

Only...could I really do that?

Could I really give up on a girl who was so wonderful, both as a woman and as a human being?

"Oh, by the way, where's Ayase?" I asked. "Is she still in her room?"

"I think she'll be home soon," Akiko replied.

"So she's out. That's unusual."

"Yes, it is. It's been months since she last—... Oh, speak of the devil."

We heard the front door open, followed by the sound of footsteps proceeding down the hall.

"It's been months since she last did wha—?" I didn't finish what I was saying.

The answer had appeared before me, and I no longer needed to ask.

"Hi, Mom. Hi, Dad," Ayase said in a voice like water filtered till it was transparent. The girl before me was supposed to be Saki Ayase. But I couldn't be sure, because she didn't look like the Saki Ayase I knew.

"Hi, Saki," said Akiko. "Oh, what a lovely new style!"

"Hi, Saki!" Dad chimed in. "Wow, you look quite different."

They were right. She'd changed.

Her long, wheat-colored hair, which she'd once called her armor, had been chopped off.

Before, it had trailed down her back, but it now cut off above her shoulders. She had gotten a medium-length layered haircut.

Her pierced earrings stood out more than they had before, perhaps because they were no longer hidden by her hair. She was like a beautiful snake, its fangs bared.

Three months.

It hit me then that only three months had passed since I first met her.

In the normal course of life, it was natural for a person's hair length to change, as well as the shape of their body and how they wore makeup. But to me, this was the first major alteration I had seen her make.

I wanted to ask, "Why now?" In novels, a girl only cuts her hair like this when she makes some major decision or she's reached a turning point in her life. Ayase's cut probably didn't mean anything, but I seemed to sense a significance to it, and it overwhelmed me.

The words I finally managed were nothing special. In fact, they were totally ordinary.

"Hi...Ayase."

"Hi, *Big Brother*."

Clearly, and without the slightest hesitation, she called me "*Big Brother*" in front of our parents.

"Saki... Did you just say...?"

"Saki...!"

Dad and Akiko's cries of joy sounded vague and hazy, as if I was hearing them from the other side of a thin wall.

For Dad and Akiko, who had been worried about the distant way we interacted with each other, Ayase's words must have sounded like an emblem of our progress as a family.

Why had she suddenly gotten a haircut?

Why had she started referring to me as her *brother*?

I could only speculate, since she hadn't explained anything. But to me, it sounded like a warning. Like she was saying:

"We're siblings. *You can't date me*, okay?"

How ironic was that? At times like this, it would be so convenient if we could be open with each other and hash things out together. And yet here I was, relieved that I didn't have to tell her how I really felt.

I needed time to come to terms with my emotions—to cool down my

feelings for her and maintain our relationship as siblings like I was supposed to.

I had to find a way to get rid of what I felt inside before Ayase caught on.

Swallowing back the desire to admire her new hairstyle, I vowed to do just that.

● EPILOGUE
SAKI AYASE'S DIARY?

This is a record of the past week.

What am I supposed to do?

I've been staring at the ceiling, thinking about things for a while now.

It is currently…four thirty-six AM.

It's still dark, since the sun doesn't rise until a little after five at this time of year.

I don't have to get up for another hour and a half. I went to bed early last night because I was exhausted, and as a result, I woke up much earlier than I thought I would.

The curtains are gently swaying at the edge of my vision. Cool air is blowing from the air conditioner without directly hitting me, keeping the room comfortable despite the rising temperature.

On the other side of the window, through the gaps between the fluttering drapes, I can see the white sky above Shibuya before dawn.

It's going to be sunny. Another hot day.

And I'm in here, thinking.

One month—I've somehow managed to endure this for a whole month.

I hated that he was making memories that I wasn't aware of. I hated that someone else knew sides to him that I didn't know.

That's not quite right. I wasn't even aware that I hated it. I just had this suffocating feeling in my heart that kept getting bigger and bigger.

What's going on?

I asked myself that one month ago and finally understood the identity of this strange emotion.

* * *

It's jealousy.

I wrote that in my diary.

And as soon as I wrote it, I finally understood.

He's always neutral with people.

That's why he can work things out with a complicated person like me—perceive me without bias, recognize the effort and the hard work I put in that I've never let anyone else see. He understands me.

I want to know him better. I want to understand him.

Yuuta Asamura.

I'm attracted to him.

But when I see how happy Mom is when she's with Dad, I can't bear to destroy that, and Asamura would be troubled if he knew how I feel.

Of course he'd be troubled.

That's why I try to act like a stranger at work.

Every time I act formal with him, like a stranger who just met him, I feel like I'm taking a step away from him. If I didn't, I'd probably start getting greedy.

And I've managed to do that for a month.

When was it that I started falling apart? I suppose it was around then.

That morning when Mom almost pulled one over on him. Despite her gentle demeanor, Mom is really good at deceiving people.

But that's okay. Asamura can't always be smart, though he usually maintains more of a cool head.

It was Dad who launched a surprise attack after that. Then Mom joined in, suggesting that I call Asamura "Yuuta."

Hold on there, Mom.

Yuuta? I could never call him that. I wonder if other siblings called each other by their first names. Do they? Is that what younger sisters everywhere call their older brothers?

I find that hard to believe.

Then leave it to Dad to add something else. He said he called my mom "Ayase" before they started dating. What a thing to say.

I'm going to remember that now every time Asamura calls me "Ayase." "Before they started dating," huh?

Dating. By "dating," do they mean…like going out together?

I was mulling over things like that when Asamura asked about my plans for the summer.

He was asking indirectly if I intended to go out with friends.

I reflexively said I didn't, because the day before, Maaya had invited me to go to the pool. Not only that, but she also suggested that I bring Asamura. Going to the pool would be fun. And I thought it would be even more fun if Asamura went, too.

That was all I could think about after Maaya's invitation, and I wasn't getting anywhere studying for my exams. I hadn't even completed half of what I'd planned to.

Then I noticed something else. Once I started thinking about Asamura, he was all I could think about. I couldn't focus on my work at all.

I've always had my mind set on becoming independent so that I won't be a burden on Mom. To do that, I have to maintain my current grades. I'm not as smart as Asamura, which means I have to spend more time on my studies.

That's why I had to turn down the offer to go swimming. I even went all the way to his room to tell him.

I was glad he believed it when I said Maaya and I weren't the type of friends who got together during summer break. I wasn't sure what to do if that didn't convince him.

I was still worried, though, that he may have seen through my lie and realized I was panicking. He notices all sorts of things.

It took him no time to locate a book I couldn't find after more than ten minutes of searching. That was amazing. The customer was delighted.

Then he said *she* would have found it sooner.

Shiori Yomiuri.

I didn't like hearing him praise her and hated myself for it. How selfish am I?

But then on our way home, I realized there are things that even Asamura isn't good at.

That was fun.

The next day, the air conditioner in our living room stopped working.

I stayed in my room till it was time to leave for work since I can't take the heat.

I kept the air conditioner on full blast and tried to catch up on my studies, listening to lofi hip-hop on my headphones.

But I didn't get anywhere.

I left for work after the heat peaked and sat in a café until it was time to clock in.

I ordered a Frappuccino since I had a 50 percent discount coupon and read while I cooled off. I was in the middle of the book that Asamura recommended. I stood up when it was time to go and saw Asamura sitting in the same café.

I greeted him on impulse.

But there were two drinks on his table, which meant he was with someone...

As we talked, a well-built boy in glasses came toward us. I knew he went to our high school and was close with Asamura, so I abruptly ended our conversation and left.

We acted like strangers at school. We didn't need to give away our secret right there.

But okay. So the drink belonged to that boy.

I was a little relieved.

I went straight to work after that, and the only people on shift were Asamura, Yomiuri, me, and a full-time employee.

Yomiuri praises me every time I see her. She says I'm a fast learner and have tremendous talent. I can tell she means it. She's a great mentor.

She's mature, beautiful, easy to get along with, and takes care of people.

To think that a woman like her has been at Asamura's side all this time...

That evening, it happened.

Asamura asked me *that* question—whether Maaya had invited both of us to the pool.

My heart leaped.

How did he know?

I don't even want to think about my reaction.

It was definitely suspicious.

For a minute there, I wondered if Maaya had reached out to him directly. I would have realized if I kept a cool head that they weren't in contact.

I wondered if Asamura wanted to go.

If he did, then he might hate me if he found out that I'd already turned down the invitation. I mean, going to a pool during summer break? Of course I wanted to go. I hadn't been to a pool in years.

But…

…I had enough trouble making progress studying. I didn't have the time for fun and games.

I was sure of it.

"No? Then you don't need to force yourself." (Because I'm not supposed to be having fun.)

"I'm not going." (I can't go.)

It was as if my inner voice were echoing on a second channel, piling up like snow and turning into ice…

My heart must have been at its limit.

I got up early the next morning, not wanting to see Asamura.

I finished making breakfast before he was up, then quickly locked myself in my room. As long as I texted him to say breakfast was ready, there would be no problem.

He sent me a curt thank-you message. He didn't add a sticker or emoji. Was it because I didn't, either? He's good at coordinating and always goes along with what I do.

But was that what he really wanted? Maybe he enjoyed using fun stickers like other people. If he did, then he should just do it. He didn't need to copy me.

Other people—like Shiori Yomiuri, for example.

Maybe it was because I was lost in thought that it took me a few moments to hear the knocking at my door.

I quickly removed my headphones and opened the door a crack.

As I had expected, it was Asamura, and he brought up the subject of going to the pool again.

I sounded like I was giving him the cold shoulder because I didn't want to hear about it anymore. But for once, he was being forceful.

He asked for Maaya's contact information.

Why had I acted like that?

I can't believe the words of rejection that came out of my mouth.

I was awful.

I sounded like an immature child.

My blood turned cold for just a moment when I saw the surprise on his face. I realized I had no right to treat him that way.

I somehow managed to settle down.

He was right to ask for her contact info. She'd asked him to go, too, after all. I couldn't just refuse. Still, I didn't think it was right to simply hand over the info without Maaya's permission. I told him that, and he backed off.

I had to ask Maaya if it was okay to give him her contact info.

But she said she was away on a trip.

Would I annoy her if I called or texted her while she was busy enjoying herself?

I knew these were all excuses, but that didn't matter.

That had been a truly bad day. I didn't think Asamura was acting that way on purpose, but he kept doing things that shook me up. He even came to work with Yomiuri.

I hated that he forced me to tackle my feelings—what I didn't like—head-on.

I mean, he was free to do whatever with whomever.

Yomiuri with her long, ladylike black hair. She's lovely, even to my eyes, and she's a wonderful match for Asamura's down-to-earth vibes.

I wonder if maybe Asamura likes beautiful, long black hair.

I have long hair, too, though it's a different color.

...What am I thinking? Geez. I feel like an idiot.

That day, I was afraid to see Asamura again and took off on my own after finishing my shift, leaving him a message that I had some shopping to do.

I went home after finishing, and there he was, standing in the kitchen.

I realized then that I had left without preparing dinner. He turned around, noticing that I was home, and looked confused for some reason, holding a pack of frozen rice and vegetables in one hand.

Seeing him standing there with the rice like that made me chuckle...

For a boy in today's world, he knows so little—almost nothing—about cooking.

It's probably because of his mother.

From what he's told me, it sounds like he didn't have any home-cooked meals after his dad became a single parent. He never learned how to cook. But I think it's more than that—I think he didn't want to learn, because of his mother. There are plenty of opportunities to see home-cooked meals these days, after all.

Yet here he is, trying hard to learn.

It was fun to prepare dinner.

Asamura always gives me a helping hand. It felt like we were cooking together.

But after dinner, he sighed and brought up *that* subject again.

About going to the pool.

Why did he sigh? I remember that it irritated me.

No longer able to take it, I picked up my phone and was about to look up Maaya's contact info.

I hadn't even messaged her yet.

But Asamura stopped me and said it didn't matter.

Not only that, but he also said that he wanted *me* to have fun at the pool.

I was at a loss for words.

Why was he worried about whether *I* had fun?

I asked him that, and he said he was concerned about me. He wanted me to cut myself more slack and have more fun.

But I have to study. I have no time for fun and games.

Because if I don't…I'll be useless.

That night, I kept thinking about it until one, then two in the morning, and I couldn't focus on my studies. I gave up and got into bed, but Asamura's words kept ringing in my mind.

I wondered why he'd said the things he said.

Two months have already passed since Mom and I moved into this apartment back in June. I thought about all the things that have happened since, then remembered his words again.

I tried turning out the lights, but then memories floated up in the darkness like a mirage.

Then, when the patch of sky I could see through the gap in my drapes started to grow light, I fell asleep at last.

Behind my closed eyelids, I saw Asamura sighing. Then my mom's face overlapped with his image.

I remembered that look.

There was this one time in junior high when she suggested going to the beach. Considering our financial state, I thought there was no way that we could afford it, and I didn't want her to go out of her way to take a day off. I said I had to study and rejected the idea.

It was the same expression she'd had then—that slightly upset look.

I had held back on her account, yet I seemed to have upset her. I couldn't figure out why she was making that face.

I slept like I was in a coma.

It felt like right as I closed my eyes, I was awake again…

Sluggishly getting changed, I realized I had stopped thinking. What was it that had been troubling me?

Oh well… Whatever.

Still zoned out and unable to get my mind to work, I got dressed, went to the living room, and saw that Asamura was already up. I thought it was unusual for him to be awake so early, then looked at the clock and was shocked to see what time it was.

Staggering, I tried to go into the kitchen, and then Asamura stopped me, saying he'd fix breakfast.

I couldn't let him do that.

It was my mistake. I couldn't violate our agreement just because I'd slept badly.

But Asamura scolded me like he would a child.

Still half asleep, I could barely argue. I meekly took a seat as I was told and let him take care of breakfast.

I spread butter on the burnt toast he handed me and placed a slice of slightly charred ham on top of it.

I smelled the aroma of bread and meat, and my stomach growled. I panicked, hoping he hadn't heard it. I think I finally realized then that I was hungry.

As I waited for Asamura to sit down, he asked me a question.

Did I want hot milk? ...It made no sense.

With my mind still foggy, I asked him why I would drink something like that on a hot summer morning.

He said it would help me sleep if I went back to bed.

He warmed the milk just for me.

My body started feeling more awake as I munched quietly on my toast.

I finished eating and sipped the milk he had heated for me.

It was warm.

My body was cooled by the air from the AC, but the milk warmed up my insides.

I exhaled and felt lighter—in both mind and body.

"I've been thinking..."

Oh, whatever.

"...I don't mind going to the pool."

As soon as I said it, I felt a weight lift off my chest.

But there was one problem.

Both Asamura and I were working on the day Maaya had specified.

I slept for a couple of hours before leaving for work.

Asamura said he would leave early so he could ask the manager to change our shifts, so naturally, I told him I'd go, too. Then he said we could go to work together and pushed his bike to match my stride.

All I knew about working I'd learned from helping my mom at home, so I was worried, wondering if it was possible to negotiate and have our shifts changed.

As I panicked on our way to work, Asamura taught me how to negotiate.

Thanks to him, our discussion with the manager went well. We were allowed to switch our shifts with someone else, and we bowed gratefully to the manager.

Again, I thought Asamura was amazing.

I could never accomplish something like that.

Maybe he was a better communicator than he thought.

I told him that, and he said I gave him too much credit. He said you were expected to be sincere at work, and that made things easy.

I understood right away.

It was the same as the two of us hashing things out.

Looking at it that way, it was easy to accept. Negotiating wasn't about forcing your way to get what you wanted. It was about coordinating the preferences of both parties and finding a meeting point.

Since you were attempting to get your own way, you should also hear what the other party wanted. The weights on the balance had to be equal or else the scale would tip.

I wouldn't mind if it tipped slightly in the other person's favor, though.

I liked to give more when it came to give-and-take. It wasn't a problem for me if the other person was at a slight advantage.

If that's acceptable, then maybe I can also try to be like Asamura.

The manager told us to work hard, and I felt confident I could do just that.

I texted Maaya as soon as we knew we could make it and told her that Asamura and I would take part.

Less than a minute later, she texted me with a thumbs-up sticker, and I was smiling as a lengthy message came in.

This is what it said in the subject line: Let's Make Summer Memories! Schedule.

...Was that what she'd been doing during her trip?

Okay. Whatever.

Then the next morning—yesterday—Asamura said he only had the swim trunks he used in PE, and he was hesitant to wear them to the pool. He said he'd go out and buy a new swimsuit after work.

What should I do? I have a swimsuit. I'd found a cute one on sale when I went to buy my school swimsuit.

Our financial situation had improved considerably by the time I enrolled in high school (I would never have gotten into Suisei otherwise), and I had some money, so I couldn't stop myself from taking advantage of the sale.

That was when I was just starting high school—more than a year ago.

But...I haven't had a single chance to wear it.

I tried it on after receiving Maaya's message yesterday, but it was a little snug, and the pattern didn't really match my current style.

So I started looking for a new swimsuit online until I had to leave for work. Since I have a job now, I can afford it.

Once our shift was over, I asked Asamura where he planned to go shopping.

The department store he mentioned carried the brand that I was after, so I said I'd go with him.

Once we got there, I wondered what kind of swimsuit he would choose but quickly shook off the thought.

What good would it do to think about that? I couldn't exactly tag along while he shopped.

Of course I couldn't.

The escalator took him farther away toward the upper floor.

I hope he didn't notice that I was panicking. He looked perfectly calm. And here I was, all flustered. It felt a little unfair.

Today was the day.

It was fun! So, so fun!

A pool for the first time in years!

There were tons of attractions, and I got to swim a lot!

I had talked to some of the people in our group, and I recognized some faces, but I've never been very good at making friends.

I'm not good at reading the room, and I don't like being asked to match other people's energy.

But it wasn't so bad today.

I think it's because Asamura was there.

He doesn't go along with Maaya's antics, either, but he's better at handling those types of situations than I am. He can manage it if he wants to.

But he's clear about what he doesn't like.

That's why I'm attracted to him.

We said good-bye to the others at Shinjuku Station.

Maaya called out to Asamura as we were leaving.

She wanted to share contact info, and for some reason, he glanced my way.

I averted my eyes.

Why did he look at me? He can do whatever he wants.

It was his decision.

By the time I looked back, they had finished swapping info, and Asamura was thanking her for setting up the event.

I listened and realized how carefully Maaya had planned everything.

Maaya Narasaka may be physically small, but she has a big heart.

She must really like people.

She has a wide range of friends, as if she likes diversity itself.

Not me. I'm really picky about people. The minute I start disliking someone, I shut them out.

I wonder how many of the people I saw today I could go out with again, and I was sickened by my lack of enthusiasm. How selfish am I?

The reason I don't like going out with people is because I'm afraid they'll see through me and realize how selfish I am.

I don't want to make people uncomfortable. That isn't fair. It isn't their fault. I just can't accept them.

So I'm impressed when I watch Asamura.

When we played that game that Maaya set up, he didn't think about standing out in the group. All he thought about was making sure that everyone else had fun. He pays attention to other people and the effort they put in.

I thought he was cool, though no one else seemed to notice.

Was I the only one who saw him? That made me kind of proud.

And scared.

Later, we walked home together.

It was just the two of us.

It was getting dark, and it was hard to make out his face as he walked next to me.

He probably couldn't see my face, either.

I thought now was the time to say it.

He was so bright, I felt blinded. He looked so cool.

And so...

Big Brother.

I said it loud and clear.

My heart wouldn't stop thumping.

I hope he didn't notice that my fingers were shaking.

I have to tell myself that we're siblings.

But I don't want to distance myself from him, either. I don't want to hurt his feelings when he's trying to be a good brother.

We had dinner together when we got home.

Watching him enjoy his meal made me realize why Mom always enjoys cooking for me.

I wonder if I looked like that when I drank the milk that he heated for me.

I told myself that the pleasure I felt was strictly that of a younger sister.

I chose my next words carefully so he wouldn't realize how I felt.

"Do you want more miso soup?"

He answered, "*Nah… Thanks, Ayase.*"

I felt his eyes on me and thought, *Crap*.

It seemed like he wasn't talking about the miso soup.

Maybe I'm too self-conscious. Maybe it was just wishful thinking, an embarrassing delusion.

But in Asamura's gaze, I thought I saw the kind of emotion he might feel about a girl—not about his sister.

…I'm sorry, Asamura. I'm just seeing my own thoughts reflected in your eyes. You wouldn't make a mistake like that.

But what if?

What if he loves me? What if he tells me that he loves me? What would happen then?

Would I be able to reject him like I should?

I'm scared.

If I'm the only one who's broken, I can keep these emotions locked away and pretend forever that I haven't noticed them.

But if he took that first step? I couldn't bear it. I would fall apart completely.

The next day, I got up when the alarm on my bedside table started ringing.

I went to the living room and saw that Mom and Dad were up.

They appeared to have taken the day off, saying it was a chance for the whole family to relax together.

Mom looked happier than she'd ever been.

I'm so glad for her. Now she won't have to suffer like she did before. I wanted her to have lots of joy in her life to make up for the hardships she'd been through in the past.

So.

I'll bury my feelings deep inside.

I don't want to ruin her and Dad's happiness. I don't want to trouble Asamura.

Please, God, don't let anyone notice my feelings.

I'll get my hair cut.

Once I made the decision, I quickly took action.

Beautiful long hair like Shiori Yomiuri had—it was a mark of femininity and one of the elements that drew Asamura to her.

I knew a haircut wasn't going to solve my problems. But I had to do everything I could to prevent cracks from forming in our relationship.

What a joke.

Ironically, I'm the one who's most affected by stereotypical images of femininity and masculinity. I always hated that about myself.

I got my hair cut and returned home.

I pulled my diary out of my desk drawer and read what I'd written to date.

I realized I'd been writing more honestly than I'd thought.

Every word, every sentence—it all laid out how I'd become more and more attracted to him.

But I haven't put into words the things that happened over the past week.

Nope. My diary entries this week only exist in my head.

Why is that? The answer…is simple.

I can't take even the slightest chance of Asamura reading this.

I finally realized the risks of keeping a diary. There's no guarantee that he won't come across it if I leave these thoughts in writing.

I'll throw it away. And then I will never, ever write down my emotions on paper. I'll stick to revisiting memories only in my head.

I must hide my girlish feelings. I can't interact with him as a regular girl. I have to be his stepsister.

I have no more need for a diary to record my days as his stepsister.

AFTERWORD

Thank you for picking up Volume 3 of *Days with My Stepsister*. I'm Ghost Mikawa, and I wrote the YouTube and novel versions of this story. Volume 3 is a crucial volume where a major change occurs in the minds of Yuuta Asamura and Saki Ayase, who have been trying to maintain an appropriate distance from each other. My editor and the anime staff have given me their approval, saying it's a divine masterpiece, but I wonder how you, my readers, feel about it. Nothing would please me more than if you gave it your seal of approval as well.

As you may be aware if you've already read the main story, another meaning I put into the title, *Days with My Stepsister*, becomes evident in this book, and the story will take a turn from here on out. Of course, the idea of showing the characters' everyday lives with care will remain unchanged, but the stepsiblings' relationship couldn't possibly stay the way it has been so far…as suggested in the final part of this volume.

The new characters who made casual appearances in this episode will be part of further developments, so please look forward to finding out what roles they have to play. I hope you will continue to watch over the stepsiblings and how their relationship develops.

Thank you.

As always, I extend my gratitude to Hiten, the illustrator, for her lovely illustrations. I can't thank her enough for the wonderful images she has created for the scenes in this story. I particularly like the cover art for this volume. It gives me a curious sense of nostalgia to see the two characters chatting as they walk along a street at night. It isn't as if I share the same type of memory from my youth, but my brain immediately fabricated a false one as soon as I saw the illustration. Combined with the meaning of the scene as it comes up in the book, I think it's one of the best illustrations yet, and I look forward to more.

Yuki Nakashima, who plays Saki Ayase; Kouhei Amasaki, who plays Yuuta Asamura; Ayu Suzuki, who plays Maaya Narasaka; Daiki Hamano, who plays Tomokazu Maru; and Minori Suzuki, who plays Shiori Yomiuri: Thank you always for your lovely performances. You bring the characters to life in the anime version and give me a clearer image of them as people when I write.

Thanks also to Yuusuke Ochiai, the video director, and our staff handling the YouTube version. With your help, *Days with My Stepsister* has come this far and has the support of many readers and viewers. A big thanks to every one of you.

Last but not least, I want to express my deep gratitude to my readers and fans of the videos. Thank you for cheering on and supporting *Days with My Stepsister*. I'll do my best to make it worth rooting for, and I hope you will continue to enjoy it for a long time to come.

Yuuta has finally realized what he's feeling, and it's a feeling he shouldn't have…

How will Saki's and Yuuta's lives gradually shift…

It's been one month since Saki called him "Big Brother." Their sibling relationship seemed to be progressing well, but hidden feelings make their interactions awkward, and Yuuta starts focusing on his schoolwork and seeking new encounters in an effort to forget the love growing inside him.

Parent-teacher conferences, university visits, and coed study sessions bring new meetings for both Saki and Yuuta.

DAYS WITH MY STEPSISTER, VOL. 4

"Can you say for certain that you didn't fall in love with her just because she was the only girl nearby?"

...in the next installment of this true-to-life romance between siblings?

Will their hearts emain unchanged, even as they meet w people? In order to answer that uestion, Yuuta and aki must face their eelings once again.

The present or the future? Common sense or insanity? Truth or appearances? Their own happiness or that of the family? What should come first, and what should be left behind?

After poring over these questions and widening their social circles, Yuuta and Saki arrive at a certain *decision*...

ON SALE IN FALL 2024!

MANGA ADAPTATION
DAYS
with My
STEPSISTER

CURRENTLY
PUBLISHING!
Art by
Yumika Kanade